A HOUSE AT THE EDGE OF TEARS

Other Books by Vénus Khoury-Ghata

POETRY

Terres stagnantes
Au sud du silence
Les Ombres et leurs cris
Qui parle au nom du jasmin
Un faux pas du soleil
Monologue du mort
Leçon d'arithmétique au grillon
Fables pour un peuple d'argile
Ils
Anthologie personnelle
Elle dit
Compassion des pierres
Quelle est la nuit parmi les nuits
La Voix des arbres

FICTION

Les Inadaptés
Dialogue à propos d'un Christ
 ou d'un acrobate
Le Fils empaillé
Alma cousue main
Vacarme pour une lune morte
Les Morts n'ont pas d'ombre
Mortemaison
Bayarmine
La Maîtresse du notable
Les Fugues d'Olympia
Les Fiancées du cap Tenès
La Maestra
Privilège des morts
Une Maison au bord des larmes
Le Moine, l'ottoman et la femme
 du grand argentier
Zarife la folle et autres nouvelles

Other Books by Marilyn Hacker

POETRY

Desesperanto
First Cities: Collected Early
 Poems
Squares and Courtyards
Winter Numbers
Selected Poems 1965–1990
Going Back to the River
Love, Death, and the Changing
 of the Seasons
Assumptions
Taking Notice
Separations
Presentation Piece

TRANSLATIONS

She Says by Vénus
 Khoury-Ghata
How There Was Once a Country
 by Vénus Khoury-Ghata
A Long-Gone Sun by Claire
 Malroux
Edge by Claire Malroux
Birds and Bison by Claire
 Malroux

A House at the Edge of Tears

Vénus Khoury-Ghata

Translated by Marilyn Hacker

Graywolf Press
SAINT PAUL, MINNESOTA

Publication of this volume is made possible in part by a grant provided
by the Minnesota State Arts Board, through an appropriation by the
Minnesota State Legislature; a grant from the Wells Fargo Foundation
Minnesota; and a grant from the National Endowment for the Arts,
which believes that a great nation deserves great art. Significant support
has also been provided by the Bush Foundation; Target, with support
from the Target Foundation; the McKnight Foundation; and other generous contributions from foundations, corporations, and individuals. To
these organizations and individuals we offer our heartfelt thanks.

MINNESOTA   NATIONAL
STATE ARTS BOARD   ENDOWMENT
                   FOR THE ARTS

A Lannan Translation Selection
Funding the translation and publication of exceptional literary works

Published by Graywolf Press
2402 University Avenue, Suite 203
Saint Paul, Minnesota 55114
All rights reserved.

www.graywolfpress.org

Published in the United States of America
Printed in Canada

ISBN 1-55597-434-1

2   4   6   8   9   7   5   3   1
First Graywolf Printing, 2005

Library of Congress Control Number: 2005925172

Cover design: Kyle G. Hunter
Cover photograph: © Corbis

The house was at the edge of the road as if
at the edge of tears
its windowpanes ready to burst into sobs.

The same wind that comes from the sea has run down the same streets for forty years. The rain that used to drench the buildings crosses a field of ruins. At the two extremities of this field: a house where my father conducted a reign of terror and a grave where he found a place not meant for him. He was buried there by chance. War had scrambled the country's geography: the dead were given up to the closest cemetery.

Two hundred kilometers and more than thirty villages separate him from my mother, born in a village in North Lebanon. Forty years later, I keep asking myself the same question: how did these two come to hate each other so deeply after having once loved?

I exhume two of my dead and one living-dead: my brother who concentrated within himself all of his father's ambitions and fury; I want to question them, open their mouths sealed in silence, to root out by force the cause of those rages, as brutal and brief as resin-fires.

In a northern village, the tomb of a Maronite saint has been sweating blood for a century. My father's grave oozes threats from its stony pores. My mother's, modest and moss-covered, seeps tears. My mother had only her tears to defend her son. "God, let him be dead!" I would repeat until I was near fainting when my father was late coming home. I dreamed about being an orphan. Only his death would stop my mother's tears, my brother's cries of terror, and we three girls from trembling.

On the sixth of December 1950, Father, why did you throw your wife and your three daughters out into the street, keeping your son indoors to tie up on the floor like a mummy? Four faces cramped between the window's bars saw you, puffing and panting in the glimmering light of the lamp placed on the ground as you perfected your work.

—Don't kill him, my mother begged you.

—The thought of killing him never crossed my mind. I want to bury him alive.

Your threats, your son's moans, our sobs have been transformed by time into shame, a shame as penetrating as the rain that soaked the four faces fixed on your slightest movements.

Forty years later, I throw sentences on the page in great shovelfuls, with a noise of falling earth, as I dig into my shame like a grave. Why did my father play the executioner? Why did our mother weep when she should have spoken up?

Neither of the protagonists can respond. Prisoners of their death, speech was taken from them at the same time as life, and their son remembers nothing. An eighteen-year confinement in a mental hospital has diluted his memory. His memories stop at the pomegranate tree that hung over the threshold and splattered the landing with bloody juice when its fruit burst open in the sun.

To each his own tomb: mine is in these pages. Your name, Mother, is black handwriting on a stone covered in snow six months of the year. I call on you, taking care to enunciate the syllables, and you come toward me without using your crutches; you stop behind me, read over my shoulder the sentences that tell your story in a language you never mastered.

You spoke it so badly that your daughter blushed when you spoke up at school parents' meetings.

Shame at my mother's "Lebanofrench," at my father's rages, which roused our neighbors from their beds and lined them up facing our door. Shame above all at our thwarted love for that man and that woman who are now turning to dust at the two extremities of the country. Shame at displaying my shame on a page for as long as I have been writing books.

I swallow my shame as I once swallowed the food my mother cooked. Her vegetables were shut in a steamer like our cries, her oversalted salads probably seasoned with her tears.

When the dinner hour arrived, she would call us from the kitchen window facing the evening that made the nettles in the garden and the lowest branch of the pomegranate tree shiver. Only these have survived the seventeen years of war. In the razed house, someone is crying within the vanished walls. The six protagonists curse and insult one another across the disappeared window bars. The father and the son within, the mother and three daughters outside. I ask the two dead, the living-dead, and the three survivors to pick up their cues, speak their lines where they left them forty years ago. I wait for words and I hear sobs. My mother weeps in the evening, in the morning, in winter and in summer, weeps on my hand as it writes.

Pitying looks from the neighbors the next morning. Their children avoid us on the way to school and tell their friends about our cries in the night, your martyrdom and your mother's entreaties.

—Don't kill him, she kept repeating.

I didn't take part in the other children's games, that day or the days after. I stopped playing at the age of nine. Shame nailed me to the ground. Recess—that was for normal children. I made the excuse that my knees were weak, limped to prove my good faith, still limp out of habit.

A cemetery's silence, in the evening, at home. Your mother's lips blue, as if she had been eating blackberries; blue, too, the rope marks around your neck. You wear them with pride, like a saint his stigmata. Suddenly, a tango melody escaping from a neighboring window etches a blindly blissful smile on your swollen lips. You get up like a bird ready to take flight. You move away from the spot where you knew humiliation and fear. You are deaf to your little sister's sobbing. Mina weeps for no reason. The violin saws at her heart and last night has left her with delicate nerves. The phonograph of Madame Alma, director of the Universal Tango Institute, is your only way to leave these walls soaked through with your sweat and your blood. The music stops, you are among us again, and immerse yourself in your homework. You work in semidarkness; the second lamp that lit the living room was broken yesterday when your father tied you up on the ground.

Seated on the doorstep, my mother scrutinized the darkness, searching for a silhouette. She made a place for me beside her and explained that I ought not to hold a grudge against my father.

—He is clumsy. He doesn't know how to express his affection. It's because of grave events that go back to his childhood in a country beyond the border.

Her hand swept the north behind her shoulder.

—No one, she added, ever knew where they came from, the woman and the two boys who got out of a cart on the square of a southern village. Had they chosen the place for the shade of its plane trees or for the gaping doorway of the church? That woman, was she a widow, or was she fleeing from a too-brutal husband, an assassin perhaps? Bent over the washtub of the monastery where she had taken refuge, she still had the bearing of a queen. Her meager wages permitted her to pay for her elder son's schooling; she ceded the younger to the monks. He would take the habit. Such a secretive woman: she never referred to her daughter kept behind by the irascible father, a daughter whom she would find again twenty years later, dressed in the traditional garments of peasant women from the plains that supply Syria with its wheat, the dress of seasonal workers traveling with the harvests from all over the Middle East.

My mother brought the shame forward from generation to generation, right up to the doorstep where she waited.

—And the young monk?

My voice startled her. She had forgotten my presence, so preoccupied with reconstructing the family of the man she had married.

—The young monk broke his vows after his return from Rome. In the hospital with appendicitis, he met me. He married his nurse. The doctorate in theology wasn't good for much. He had to find other prospects. He became an interpreter under the French mandate, the army absorbed him after the French left. A mystic in a world of brutes. He never recovered from it. He could have become a bishop or even a cardinal had it not been for that accursed appendicitis, which turned him away from his vows. An orphan of France. He threatened every morning to blow his brains out. An invisible hand held him back at the last moment. He didn't have the right to attempt suicide; he was the father of five children, four girls and a boy.

—Three girls, I felt obliged to remind her.

—Four, she insisted. The eldest died at the age of eight months. She broke her father's heart and made him doubt God. He wrote a long poem for her funeral with lines of the same length and the same width. You ought to have seen him gesticulate above the little coffin. The few neighbors who had accompanied us to the cemetery could barely keep from laughing. His voice trembled in the wind. A glacial day. The gravedigger worked like a dog digging into the frozen ground. His spade in the air, he waited for the end of the poem to fill up the hole. That man is jinxed, the curse will follow him from life to life. He took advantage of the poor monks, ate the monastery's bread with impunity. When he had finished his theological studies, he traded his cassock for a three-piece suit. The little one paid for his sins. Dead.

—You've never talked about her . . .

—What would be the use!

—Do you have a photo of our sister?

—A photo, a photo! That's easy to say. You needed an occasion: baptism, first communion. The little one didn't wait. Always sick, as if she were in a hurry to leave. I'll say it again: she had to pay for him.

—What was her name?

—How do you think I can remember it after all these years! Victoire, if my memory is right, or maybe Victorine.

A man's footsteps, recognizable among all others, made her jump. She got up, tied her apron, and disappeared into the kitchen. My father emerged from the darkness. His army boots made the gravel creak on the footpath.

"A man should refuse to live when he has planted his child under a cypress," my father would repeat, and his mouth stayed shut after prouncing the name of that funereal tree.

God had taken from him the child he loved and left the one he loathed. From where did he get this son? This unruly boy who resembles no one in the family? He is small-boned with long, silky lashes: no one but the devil could camouflage evil so seductively. Pristine features for a soiled soul: he reads books that have banished God from their pages, listens to music as black as the continent that gave it birth. A music come from far away. My father had a hard time accustoming himself to this son's presence under his roof. A question escaped from him from time to time, murmured like an insult: "Why did he choose my home rather than the Vinikofs' more spacious one? His perversity would be well adapted to their madness. His lack of austerity would go well with their appetites."

Our Sundays were dreary indeed compared with those of the Vinikofs, who lived in a well-kept building on the other side of the street. The whole family would crowd into an old Packard to go and dig for buried treasure a hundred kilometers outside Beirut. The Armenian magus who had revealed its existence to the engineer Vinikof had not been skimpy with details. One had to turn off after a bridge, follow the railroad tracks, drive through farmlands to the base of a hill, then stop in front of a tuft of broom. The bridge, the hill, and all the rest could be found on the map; all the map lacked were the railroad tracks. The Vinikofs weren't going to be dissuaded by such a small detail. They decided that the Armenian had seen the site with his third eye, and they turned south. Two adults and four children took off every Sunday under our dazzled gazes. The head of the expedition, at the wheel, wore a compass around his neck.

We would wait for their return as late as it might be, ready to spend the night on the sidewalk. The headlights of the car as it reappeared made us blink. We bombarded them with questions though they were staggering with fatigue.

—And the treasure?

They showed us their hands covered with blisters, their legs scratched to ribbons by thorns.

—But did you find it, the treasure ?

—That will be for next Sunday.

And that was their answer, for five years. At the

moment when the earth was opening beneath their pickaxes, they would hear the sound of axes like their own
striking the ground from the other side of the hill.
Blows that stopped when the Vinikofs stopped digging
and began again when they went back to work.

—Do you mean that other people are . . .

They would shake their heads in both directions: a
yes bedecked with a no.

—If you want to call devils people, they would say.

The wise man had warned their father.

—Your task, engineer, will not be an easy one. You
will have to struggle. Demons will track you down.
They will follow your every step, and will dig on their
own side. I advise you to throw them off the track, to
pretend you're giving up, to leave, since you'll have to
return when they have their backs turned, otherwise
their axe blows will always answer yours, five seconds
later, not one more.

It was astounding. Mina, who dared to suggest echoes,
was asked to keep her opinions to herself. One doesn't
contradict a magus. As to echoes, the engineer Vinikof
had certainly thought of that.

Emotion enhancing their appetites, the Vinikof family
rushed into the kitchen, where each one prepared his
or her own specialty. Fat Roro's platter of a dozen fried
eggs resembled a virgin planet scattered with craters.
Skinny Youri, who spent his time masturbating, spied
on by his two sisters, ate only asparagus and mayon-
naise. The steaming casserole placed by the mother in
the middle of the table was as deep as the baptismal font
in the parish church. What steamed within smelled of
sumac, cumin, saffron, and lamb. The ceiling sweated
copiously while the six members of the family ate. The
adults did so with appetite, the twin girls who were in

my class picked at their food. All these savory dishes only filled them with disgust. They preferred our own mother's bland and tasteless cooking. A hospital diet.

Macha and Yara had trouble getting up in the morning to go to school. I would call them by rapping three times on the window, then wait for them with my nose pressed to the pane, sometimes for more than an hour. Their disorder fascinated me. It contrasted sharply with the order that reigned in our house. The nightshirts rolled up at the foot of their beds smelled of healthy sleep. The mufflers hung from the lamp were flags at half-mast. Macha and Yara crawled under their beds to retrieve their shoes and fought like dogs for the same sock, which ended up as two half-socks, one piece gripped in each one's hand. Well-behaved Roro slept fully dressed, and Youri, who had banished socks from his life, exhibited ankles as skinny as a rooster's without embarrassment. A temporary emaciation, according to his sisters. Youri would fill out again as soon as he lost the unfortunate habit of masturbating.

Youri's masturbation—a subject for humor for the Vinikofs. Your nocturnal ejaculations, Victor, are the subject of drama in our family. Your father snatches you from sleep and then throws you outdoors for the rest of the night. You are the shame of the family. You have soiled the sheets washed by your saintly mother. The door, violently slammed, wakes the neighbors. Lined up in front of the window, they plead with your father for clemency and console your mother with inadequate words. They are all there. The show is free. Four children and two adults act out scandals to distract them. Our landlady, Madame Rose, is followed by the four racetrack brothers and their sister, Mademoiselle Renée. Madame Alma, called the Contessa, argues with Georges Vinikof in a low voice. Madame Latifa, the Muslim, stands behind them. Her religion forbids her to show herself unveiled. They sympathize with my mother while agreeing with my father in principle. What will become of us if fathers no longer have the right to discipline their children? Only Monsieur Alphonse isn't there. Our drama doesn't interest him.

The rumor, embellished with new details, travels around the neighborhood. Fabrications become evidence. You were about to rape one of your sisters, never mind which one, when your father intervened. You don't throw your son out into the street for a commonplace loss of semen. You inspire mistrust. Children run away at the sight of you and their mothers interrupt their conversations as soon as you appear. Some of them cross themselves. The retirees

*who play backgammon in front of their doorsteps forget to
throw the dice.*

*—Such a good-looking boy. What a pity that he's a
pervert.*

*All you had to do was slow down to catch the rest of
the sentence.*

*—He's paying for the sins of his father: a defrocked
monk who made use of the poor monks' generosity to go
to school and to see the world. So much for the monastery,
he married his nurse.*

*Known for her great wisdom, Madame Rose, our land-
lady, expresses herself with a proverb: Sour fruit the parents ate set the children's teeth on edge.*

*The rape story goes as far as your school, after spreading
to the Young People's Movement, thanks to which you had
discovered Beethoven, Bach, Mozart, Brahms. It's there
that you take shelter when the atmosphere at home becomes unbearable. You're now made to understand that
your presence is no longer welcome. To console you, you
are charitably given the third movement of Brahms's violin concerto, which you would listen to repeatedly when
the world around you seemed hostile. A useless gift. On
what were you supposed to play the record?*

*Witness at the trial that he had set in motion and that
was now out of his hands, your father mutely watches the
parade of teachers called upon to testify against you.*

—Scratches his crotch, says one.

*—Stares at himself incessantly in the pane of the open
window, says another.*

—Writes unrhymed poems, puts forward a third.

*The fourth one flourishes two pages covered with your
handwriting. Your last composition. Subject: Write a letter*

to your parents. Yours is addressed to your brother in Hell and Abyssinia, Arthur Rimbaud.

Your father is advised to send you away from the capital, site of all temptations, to send you to the south of the country, to a monastery known for its strict rules and its austerity. The company of the monks will be beneficial for you. The cold will cure you of your unhealthy urges. You will teach the peasant postulants and learn at the same time.

Did your mother's sorrowful gaze make the principal take pity on her? His reassuring tap on her shoulder made her let fall the tear she had been holding in the corner of her eye. She must take him for the abbot of the monastery to kiss his hand with such devotion.

This testimony against you mortified her. She almost spoke up to defend you; your father prevented her. In what language would she have spoken? Unthinkable to speak Arabic in front of the school faculty. As for her French, which we called Swahili, it would have provoked sniggering, indeed, pity.

Upon returning home, she seized the mop and washrags. She cleaned the house from top to bottom. Housework: her only therapy. She gave herself up to it with ardor when she felt herself overpowered by circumstances. She swept the dust and her worries away with the same movement, and wiped the dirt and her cares away with the same sweep of the washrag.

My mother's housecleanings are like moving out in miniature: chairs piled up on the table; armchairs hauled up on the couch; old pots, old hats, old shoes, thrown into Aunt Rose's garden, only to be taken back a few months later when autumn piles its nettles on earth split open by drought.

My mother prefers to clean at night, by the glow of the streetlight that partially lights up the rooms of our home.

She pours out buckets full of water, sweeping it outside in sprays that splash the pomegranate tree. Bent down toward the ground, she puffs and pants as if her chest harbored all the winds of the earth.

Thinking of the teachers' meeting, which had occurred that afternoon, slows her movements. She has trouble working, stops often to think things over, then unties her apron and sits down on the doorstep. Her eyes scan the neighboring buildings: they seem larger in the darkness. Daylight takes away their msytery, tamps them down.

Five houses of unequal height, built in defiance of common sense by Aunt Rose's late husband who had made a fortune in Cuba during the First World War, while his own country squirmed beneath the Turkish boot. He had even left a son on the island, a bastard born of his lovemaking with a native woman whom he did not marry. Five dwellings rather than houses, thrown together, facing each other or turning their backs, with their skylights arranged like sawteeth. Someone might build another room onto the roof, in the dark of night, right under the nose of the proprietor, who helplessly watched the transformation of her patrimony. Assessing the damage, she would utter a sentence heavy with menace: "It will be different when Candido is here."

Candido, recognized by his father on his deathbed, would inherit these walls. Aunt Rose invokes him at the end of every month, when she demands increases in rent that are refused by all her tenants. Perhaps Candido is merely their landlady's invention: the four racetrack brothers are sure of it.

As the church clock strikes twelve, your mother closes her door and goes to sleep, sitting, her head down on the wood of the table. She doesn't want to miss your departure for the center of town, where you will take the bus that makes regular trips between the capital and the southern villages.

The monastery that waits for you overlooks a hamlet of three hundred souls. It's called Machmouché. A Trappist monastery, built in the eighteenth century in the Cistercian style. From their cells, the monks have a view of the graves lined up on the hillside.

*You close the door softly behind you so as not to wake us.
You spend a whole day on roads furrowed with ice, stop-
ping in hamlets and towns with unpronounceable names.
In your canvas bag, you'd taken your pajamas, a change
of underwear, and Rimbaud. You have no idea what will
become of you up there. The other passengers stare at you.
Only the local villagers take this bus. Sometimes you doze
off, then wake with a start because of an abrupt brak-
ing. The driver shows you, pointing with his finger, walls
atop a hill. He's sorry: the bus can't go up that slope. You
walk, your back to the sun, which is setting on the other
side of a valley. You try not to lose sight of the building
planted on the hilltop like a stone flag. The road seems to
double back on itself; the monastery disappears just as
you think you're nearing it. Perhaps it's a phantom castle
that rises up before you with its black façade, its narrow
windows resembling a fortress's loopholes. Your legs, exhausted by the climb, nonetheless bring you toward the
main gate. The doorknocker leaves a layer of rust in your
palm. No one answers. You pray to God and Rimbaud
that the monastery be uninhabited.*

*Shuffling footsteps, on the other side of the gate, put an
end to your reveries. An old man's step for a youth's face.
Only the smooth cheeks and pouting mouth can be seen
beneath the hood. The young monk gestures to you to follow him. His hurricane lamp illumines walls that meet in
arches above your heads. You follow him for at least five
minutes without learning what his voice sounds like. He
stops before a door, opens it with a large key, you've never*

seen one so big; then he hands you a bowl of soup, a chunk of bread, some dried fruit.

—You'll eat alone this evening. It's past the dinner hour. The monks eat at five o'clock so as to spend the night in prayer.

His adolescent's breaking voice reminds you of an untuned piano. Your own rumbles with anger. You restrain yourself from hitting him.

—And the pupils? What the hell have I got to do with monks? I was sent to a school, not to the Trappists.

—The two aren't incompatible, he explains to you gently, his eyes fixed on the ground. You will learn obedience and you will teach us French.

A shy smile lights up his face. He pushes his hood back from his face and introduces himself:

—Brother Barnabé. Your pupils are waiting for you. We've heard that you are a poet.

He embarrasses you with the key, which he hands to you with a sweeping gesture. Is it his confidence in you that keeps you from escaping, or your legs, which refuse to take another step?

You swallow the soup and bite into the heel of bread and the dried fruit. The bed serves as a stool for you to hoist yourself up to the tiny window placed just below the ceiling. Nothing is visible at this height but a black sky replacing a gray one. You let yourself slip down onto the bed. Your hands between your legs, you curl up and squeeze your sex as if you wanted to strangle it. It's the one at fault. You're not responsible for anything. It ought to have spilled itself into the toilet, not in a bed, so close to your sleeping sister. You feel like castrating yourself.

Our home became more agreeable after my brother's departure. My father seemed less demanding, and my mother less obsessed with cleanliness. She would even occasionally sit down, smoke a cigarette, and follow the smoke with her eyes with a dreamy gaze. Her washing frenzy, which had extended even to the gravel of the walkway and the asphalt of the street when it hadn't rained for a while, diminished all at once. She would only do the dishes every three days, when the stack of plates was in danger of tumbling down. Her offhandedness was due to a new peace of mind, after her husband explained that their son was breathing fresh air, eating healthy food, living in the company of holy men, learning and teaching in God's shadow. His numerous tasks and occupations would not leave him time to masturbate. She believed him. The ex-monk who denied the body and the former nurse who reduced it to its basic functions could only agree on this subject.

Ten years later, she understood that he had tricked her. She consulted a psychiatrist. Her son was beyond recovery: too many fears, humiliations and rejections from those close to him. The psychiatrist could have cured him before he was locked up, before the electroshock treatments. He gave her back the file and closed the door behind her.

—I would have paid you, she cried out in a wretched voice.

She was choking. What could have made her son feel that he was rejected? She sat down on a bench and went through everything that had happened in thought.

The cold became more biting. She got up. Making her way home, she cleared her conscience by concluding that he had gone to the monastery of his own free will, with a letter of recommendation from the school director.

Tears blurred her vision as she remembered his return, three months after he left.

Having departed like an adult, he made himself tiny to be taken back under the paternal roof.

Your appearance in the pouring rain, at night, in the doorway, paralyzes the whole household. We would have welcomed you more warmly if your father hadn't turned pale.

He paces up and down the length of the living room. His gaze, when he fixes it on you, is as dark as the sky above the garden full of nettles. He keeps walking, unceasingly.

He neither invites you in nor drives you away. He is absorbed in the sound of his own boots whose leather he waxes at regular intervals. You both pass the night fully dressed: he paces, you stand on the doorstep, until morning, when Father, having consulted his watch, takes his kepi off its hook, places it on his head, and moves toward the door. You step aside to let him pass and he thanks you by touching the brim of his cap.

The monastery at Machmouché. No one asks you to tell about it. Nor does anyone describe to you the three months spent without you. Your father had resumed saying prayers before meals, your mother had put on lipstick and gone to call on the neighbor women who had not interested her previously. In the evening, we had prayed together, kneeling in front of the Sacred Heart hung above the parental bed. Nine Hail Marys and one Our Father. Our prayers and the Contessa's tangos met halfway between the two houses, mingling until one could not distinguish the holy words from those which were not:

> *Hail Maria de la Plata*
> *Your name is in our broken hearts*
> *Blessed art thou amongst women of easy virtue*

Jesus the fruit of our inflamed kisses
pray for us poor sinners
and forgive us our trespasses as we forgive those
*   who have forgotten us in the heat of the Pampa*
Now and at the hour of our death.
Olé

This peculiar mixture doesn't bring the slightest smile to your face. The jokes and witticisms of your sisters, who had been so bored without you, leave you indifferent. You spend your time sleeping. Only sleep is capable of erasing the black façade of the monastery, its glacial refectory, the pimply faces of the novices and the closed ones of the monks. From that gloomy building perched on a hillside in South Lebanon, you keep one souvenir, a photo, of Barnabé. "Your brother in storm and suffering" he had written on the back, in a childish hand.

He slept during the day when his father wasn't home, went out at night when his father was there, kept company with a peculiar crowd, badly dressed, unshaven, shod in sandals that exhibited their filthy toes. They went from café to atelier, followed by black-clad girls, muses or models, who could be traded for a painting, dinner in a bistro, sometimes for a boy. Until dawn, they discussed Nietzsche, God, homosexuality as a mark of genius. They all advocated rupture with Family, Society, Religion, so that the Work of Art could come to pass.

"No sculpture without brutality," said one. "No music without sarcasm," continued another. "No tragedy without humor," concluded a third. They demolished everything that reassured their next-door neighbors, the people they passed in the street, those who bought their pictures and their books. They wrecked themselves with a jazz accompaniment.

His supervision had been relaxed since his return from Machmouché, so my brother did not have to answer to anyone. He returned every morning as long as someone opened the door to him, slept elsewhere if no one answered when he rang the bell. He didn't insist, retraced his steps back to the center of town, then toward a posh neighborhood where an odd and capricious Englishwoman lived, enamored of the Orient and its lights, and whose own paintings, executed in semi-darkness, made use of two colors, gray and black. The friend who brought him to Sylvia Churchill's flat introduced him as Rimbaud. The Englishwoman made a place for him on her couch, then in her bed. She loved the shadow of his lashes on his cheeks, his hair that curled on the nape of his neck, and the way he recited his poems, a tear in the corner of his eye. She never tired of looking at his pale, crucified hands. That was her own description of them.

Reassured about her son's lot, cocooned by a rich woman in her fifties, my mother did nothing to bring him back. Still, a month later, worry impelled her to the neighborhood where the lady lived. Her shopping bag on her arm, so as not to arouse her husband's suspicions, she took the streetcar as if she were going to the souk. She made use of the nine station stops to prepare her speech. With her ear glued to the door of the one who had appropriated her son, she heard words in a language she had never heard before, which must have been English, since the mistress of the house was British. She understood that her prepared speech was useless. She left on tiptoe, her empty shopping bag hanging from her arm; later, when it was full, dragging almost to the ground. Chance brought her to the center of town, in front of the café my brother frequented. She had remembered its name, La Palette. The waiter frowned: her son rarely came around these days. She could learn more from the tall mustached fellow, a painter, he was one of the crew. Paul didn't rise to greet the haggard woman who was twisting her sweat-soaked handkerchief. His attention went rather to the carrots and leeks branching out of her shopping bag. He uttered something in a bored voice:

—He's crashing with the old Englishwoman. She must pamper him. Then he broke out in a coarse laugh.

She seemed prostrate and despondent that evening,

once she had put away the dishes and swept the kitchen floor.

—I've decided to learn English, she said, before going off to bed.

—You'd do better to learn French, Mina shot back at her. My teacher says she can't understand a word of your gibberish.

A decision of no consequence, made because of a fleeting shame. My mother learned neither English nor French; she continued to speak a jargon concocted from two languages: spoken Arabic and the colonists' language. My mother, a bilingual illiterate.

She made the rounds of your friends, three years later, to find out exactly when you'd gone off the tracks, and to know the cause of your debasement. Paul, whom she found again at La Palette, denied having told her that the Englishwoman pampered you. "More likely she exhausted him, wrung him out like a wet rag, asked him to engage in acts that disgusted him." Seeing her blush, he excused himself clumsily. He was only repeating your words, since you had confided in him.

It seems that you had sometimes forgotten about the naked woman lying beneath you, and started to count the birds lined up on the branch of the chestnut tree you could see out the window. The arrival of new birds obliged you to count them all over again. You did it ten times, fifteen times, insensible to the hand at work lower down, to the mouth that breathed you in, deaf to the voice that ordered you to clear out. You found yourself in the street again; the window, slammed shut two stories above you, made you aware of the precariousness of your situation, and the fragility of the sentiments you inspired. The street became your primary abode, and your poems your only baggage; you sat on the curb and declaimed your verses, gesticulating. Heads appeared at windows. You were keeping people from sleeping. You had been expecting applause, not these piercing voices exhorting you to make your racket somewhere else.

You waited for morning, stretched out on a bench. The idea of knocking on your father's door did not cross your mind. The coins that clinked in your pocket could pay your bus fare as far as Tantine's village. Your mother's sister, a schoolteacher for thirty years in a village in North Lebanon, always put aside half her salary.

To what arguments did you resort to relieve her of her savings? Did she really believe your tale of a Parisian editor ready to publish your poetry? She gave you twice the price of an airline ticket, with only one condition: "That you stop touching yourself, otherwise hair will grow in the palms of your hands."

Poor Tantine! Her last news was of the nocturnal ejaculation that had merited your banishment from the paternal Eden. Your hand on your heart, you swore that you would never touch yourself again. What a relief to realize that she didn't know about the Englishwoman! And how would she have heard? The snow cut her village off from the rest of the world for three months, every year.

"Love from Paris. Thank Tantine for me. Victor." My mother read the postcard three times before realizing that her son was in Paris, not at the Englishwoman's.

His choice of the Eiffel Tower, she was sure, was not by chance. The Eiffel Tower and Tantine together created a puzzle. She thought about it, asked questions left and right to find out what relationship existed between her sister and the famous French monument, then finally determined that the former dispersed knowledge to little peasants, and the latter, news to an entire people—the French. The first step taken, she passed to the second: why should he be thanking Tantine? We would have the answer three weeks later, when school closed its doors and we would go to stay with our aunt in the village she had never left.

No farewells to our landlady, she detested us; nor to the Contessa, who looked down on us; nor especially to Madame Latifa who used her radio to annoy our father: the muezzin's voice, three times a day, at the highest possible volume. Just a brief visit to Mademoiselle Renée, who would invite me to her room when she had the time, and would brush my long hair for almost an hour, before braiding it in a long tress that fell to the small of my back. My silence must have encouraged her to confide in me. She was hesitant about marrying her cousin, newly released from prison, not because of his criminal record, but because of his saroual and his tarboosh, which he was the last man in the Christian district to wear. She would have preferred that he dress like a European: three-piece suit, tie, and fedora.

She talked nonstop while admiring her masterpiece in the mirror: her hairbrush and tongue moved together. Sometimes she sang in a shrillish voice, always the same song, which concerned a princess, a braid cut off, and a betrayed love. Everyone died at the end: the only survivor was the braid, which floated on an icy river in a country of fog and snow. It was a heartrending song. I would have liked to know more about this tragic love, but I was paralyzed by shyness. Mademoiselle Renée had to stand on tiptoe to kiss me, two kisses on each cheek. I towered over her by three and one-half inches, despite being only nine years old.

Madame Alma, called the Contessa, had arrived in the country recently, just a while after Castro came to power, which was hardly the case of Monsieur Alphonse, a survivor of World War II. A former soldier for Vichy, he had decided to stay in Lebanon after the Allied victory. The defeat of his regiment at Ain Kessoué disgusted him with the military forever. He became more Arab than the Arabs, walked around in babouches, swore constantly, pissed on walls, and assiduously attended the mosque—but only the plaza in front of it, for the ablutions. Prayer was of no great interest to him. Monsieur Alphonse, who received no pension, put all his savings into prayer rugs, had hundreds manufactured with a compass sewed onto them to indicate the direction of Mecca to the faithful far from their homeland. A golden opportunity, if fate had not been against him.

—The ways of the Lord are impenetrable, he liked to repeat while he was telling his story. So impenetrable were these ways that his business partner left with the till and the rugs, and left Monsieur Alphonse with the compasses.

A few words more about Madame Alma, the Contessa. The arrival in our neighborhood of this middle-aged woman enlivened the curiosity of the locals, who decided to invite her to come to tea around Aunt Rose's garden pool.

Everyone brought his or her own chair: the armchair intended for the guest was upholstered in red velvet. She wiped it off with a handkerchief before letting her buttocks touch it, then looked us over, adults and children, with her eagle eye. We inspired only her disdain, while she dazzled us with her shiny black stockings, her thick chignon crossed and held by pearly needles, her narrow heels. For the first time, we saw her up close. Madame Latifa's children lifted up her pleated skirt to see if she were made like themselves. She was. Their mother hovered over her, serving her coffee, which the Contessa made the error of drinking down to the last drop, chewing the grounds, then showing her black tongue. After turning the cup over, Madame Latifa attempted to read the grounds.

—I don't want to know, interrupted the superstitious Contessa, but Madame Latifa had already gotten started.

—By Allah, but you have many enemies! They watch your comings and goings, note your slightest gestures. But you can turn them round your little finger like a ring. Say: Inshallah!

The Contessa, who neither knew how, nor cared to say Inshallah, got up, ready to leave. Madame Latifa caught up with her. What she was going to say to her could change her life.

—Be generous to those around you, she went on, in a soothsayer's voice. Open your heart and your purse to them. They will repay you a hundredfold. Small gifts bring friendship with them. Say: Inshallah!

Before she had finished her sentence, her four kids held their hands out toward the stranger. On their grimy palms, they had drawn five-piastre coins.

A fiasco, that first visit, which was also the last. The pomegranates that we had peeled for her grated her tongue. The housewives' advice as to where to buy lentils at the best price and chickpeas for next to nothing irritated her. She led them to understand that she had no intention of opening a grocery, but would be starting a dancing school. She arose, very dignified, and called her dog, whom she had made the mistake of leaving in our care. Falstaff had not appreciated the bath we had forced him to take in Aunt Rose's pool. He had changed color, was now green where he had been white. He smelled of fish. Holding her nose with two fingers, his mistress went home, having decided never to accept another invitation from us. The Contessa hardly ever went out. Her days and her evenings were entirely given over to teaching those whom the war had made rich to dance. She worked twelve months out of twelve. *The Universal Tango Institute* was open even in summer, when the heat drove the city-dwellers out of the capital, toward holiday spots in the mountains.

At the beginning of July, we left Aunt Rose, Madame Latifa, Monsieur Alphonse, the racetrack brothers, Mademoiselle Renée, order, discipline, concrete and asphalt, for the fields, fruit eaten directly from the trees, liberty. Tantine, who had been looking out for the bus from the road's first turn into the village, was sitting in front of the cemetery gate, and she opened her arms wide to greet the three city girls. We were the daughters of her heart. She turned us loose in the countryside with the village children who asked us the same questions year after year.

—Is there snow in Beirut?

—Do you have goats in Beirut ?

—And a river? Is there a river in Beirut?

—Who needs a river when we've got the sea! And why have goats when milk comes in bottles from the grocery?

We had shamed them. We could see it on their gloomy faces. But there was always a clever one who spoke on behalf of the others. All right for the sea, for the milk in bottles, but not for the rest. We didn't have any saints or hermits.

Tantine's village had as many saints as it had goats. Each hamlet had its own, embalmed in a golden reliquary. The one at Hasroun cured the one-eyed; the one at Ehden was reputed to cure blindness. We thought Saint Saba must have been hard of hearing when we saw the number of deaf people who crowded the plaza in front of his church every Sunday.

A village so high up, it seemed to have leaped onto a cloud and to have set itself up there, with its cedars.

At its peak, a poet, Khalil Gibran, buried in the crevice of a boulder. At its base, a river, the Kadicha, whose noise drowned out the sound of church bells, the crowing of the cocks, and the howls of hyenas at night in the cemetery. In between the two were houses pressed up close against each other and the school where Tantine taught all the classes at once. The littlest ones traced their letters while the medium-sized ones did their sums and the biggest ones sweated over a dictation. Sucking their tongues in concentration, they wrote on school desks made by my uncle, the carpenter.

Tantine counted us every evening to make sure none of us had been carried away by the river or eaten by the wolf that everyone talked about but no one had ever seen: only foxes got along well in that village renowned for its women and its hens, equally plump.

My mother's news was sparse, passed from mouth to mouth until it reached the village: she distrusted the mail, capable of letting her letter go astray, and the postman, who might misquote her words. She refused to leave Beirut: her son, who hadn't shown a sign of life since he left for Paris, might return at any moment. It was from her we learned that the Vinikofs had denied themselves any vacation in order to dig every day of the week, even when the temperature reached 100 degrees in the shade. They had found a new method of working: while half the family toiled with shovels and pickaxes, the others distracted the devils by banging on pots and pans, ringing little bells, and by placing beefsteaks here and there on the ground, along with loukoum, much savored by little demons.

In Tantine's village, every week had seven Sundays. We rushed through our vacation homework to devote ourselves to clambering up and down the rocks, and to games of hide-and-seek in our uncle the carpenter's workshop on rainy days. The coffins lined up against the walls provided the best hiding places. Uncle Nicholas made them for all North Lebanon: standard ones for ordinary mortals, made-to-measure ones with goosefeather headrests for the well-to-do, and special ones with air vents for the claustrophobic.

The pencil behind his ear fell of its own will onto the notebook where he jotted down his clients' dimensions. He refused no requests, and the most extravagant demands became reasonable the moment a client paid him. He only put in his own word as to the color of the lining: his preference was for ivory, which lightened the complexion.

We would pass in silence from one coffin to another, terrified at the thought that we might be caught by the master of the premises. The sound of his footsteps caused some of us to lock ourselves in. The local constable's son passed a whole night there. He beat on the coffin lid till dawn. My uncle pulled him out, livid. He fell out with the whole band of us, cloistered himself at home, studied day and night to escape the boredom and kill time, and eventually became a doctor.

Ten years later, all the village bowed down when he passed. Great and small addressed him as Doctor. He cared for the rich and the poor, the ignorant and those who were less so, even the donkeys and the goats; but he refused to touch my uncle. He gave Tantine the priest's address when she knocked on his door one night.

—The man of God will know how to cure renal colic, he said, and shut his door. He could not forget how he had been treated by the carpenter ten years earlier. He had expected pity, not that heavy palm which struck his cheek, nor those fingers which dragged him out of the box like a dead rat and threw him onto the hedge of prickly pears.

It took us three months to forget our screaming in the night, the neighbors lined up outside our window, our brother mummified, and the terrible face of our father. The tree branches flexed beneath our weight; the goats let us drink their milk straight from the teat; only the dogs resisted us. They bore no relation to city dogs: they were only good for barking. They were the only ones to hold out against the stink of cannabis that pervaded the air from mid-August on. The only ones to walk in a straight line without zigzagging. Harvested, dried on the rooftops, cannabis produced a flameless combustion inhaled by everything that breathed. Men and beasts alike dozed. Incapable of flight, the birds walked along with heavy steps, and the snakes coiled in holes and cracks didn't resist the sticks we proffered to them. We paraded them like trophies from the dry-goods and notions shop to the grocery, then to the bookshop that sold week-old newspapers. The merchants took flight, leaving their counters at the mercy of pilferers. The priest himself was at the mercy of those torpid fumes. He declared a miracle every day at noon, when the sun reflected his skullcap in the vicarage well. The luminous circle deep in the water was Saint Anthony's halo. He instructed us to kneel down and start chanting "Our Father," without which Saint Anthony would disappear, which he did without fail as soon as the sun descended from the height of the sky.

North Lebanon: a country made of peaks and chasms. A stone hat: the Qornet-el-Sadwa, our highest point; a fault line incised by the devil's hand: the valley of the Kadicha, with its thousand-year-old grottoes, which had sheltered the Crusaders on the way to Jerusalem— Crusaders who spilled their seed in the wombs of our ancestresses, lost in admiration of their gleaming armor. The hermits who succeeded them in those rocky crevices nourished themselves on roots and grasshoppers, and flagellated themselves on Fridays in front of a crowd of believers from all over the world. On the other days of the week, they dug their graves, where they slept when it snowed. One young anchorite, who had renounced the world after being disappointed in love, behaved like a capricious celebrity. He would bless his admirers with one hand on his heart. He refused gifts of money, preferring sweets, especially milk chocolate. He had made a vow of chastity, not of austerity, and no one raised the slightest objection. Another, whose tomb began to bleed a hundred years after his death, was beatified by the Pope barely ten years ago. The Father Superior accepted all donations left in front of the church, but was beside himself with rage at the mere sight of a candle: the odor of melted wax made him sneeze. All candles were violently trampled underfoot. His church's wealth increased daily.

Tired of waiting for your return in a city suffering a heat wave and deserted by its inhabitants, your mother joins us, and the very next day goes on a pilgrimage to see the young anchorite, rumored to be able to cure madness. Had her instincts whispered to her that you'd end up in a madhouse? Her second visit is to the tomb of the poet, buried according to his wishes in those woods where he had played as a child. He had died in Boston; his homecoming in a sealed coffin, held aloft by mourners, moved the heart of the crowd and made you leap for the first time in your mother's womb. The author of The Prophet, *second only to the Bible in its number of readers, had marked your fate even before you were born. His house, restored by the town council, is next door to Tantine's. Furnished with a writing desk, a narrow bed, and a rocking chair that moves in the slightest wind, it seems to be inhabited. The dead poet rocks in his chair, blows out the candles placed in the corners one after another, and smiles wanly at those with their faces glued to the single window.*

You had renounced prose after reading his books. Even your school essays were written in alexandrines. You were last in your class: no good at math, hopeless in chemistry and physics, even in grammar, and your poems were full of grammatical and spelling errors.

Your father declared war on anything that counted out twelve feet. Searches were carried out at night, in your notebooks, your first drafts, even the white spaces that could have been written on in invisible ink. Your lines of verse were decoded word by word:

"I love the night of your face and the stars of your eyes"
made your father suspicious:

—This is about a Negress, if I understand correctly?
You had no idea how to answer.

A dictionary thrown at your head met up with the lamp
and broke it, the second one in two weeks. The spilled oil
sparked off the beginning of a fire that brought out all
the neighbors. Monsieur Alphonse snickered, Aunt Rose
fanned herself with a calendar, Madame Latifa threw
buckets of water out her window blindly, her unveiled face
not permitting her to show herself.

—Go away! There's nothing to see!

After they returned home, they must have wondered
why there was a revolver placed on our kitchen table. Did
disciplining a son necessarily require the use of firearms?

We were a disgrace. Only our mother's tears inspired respect. They were her mute language, her only source of rea-
soning, the screen behind which she took shelter. She spoke
as little as possible, never sang, but wept every time the
occasion presented itself, silent tears that flowed distinctly
on her cheeks. My mother never mixed up her tears.

Madame Latifa, who found you shortly afterwards asleep
with your back up against the chicken house, offered you
her hospitality for the night. Your father would have done
better to wait for morning to throw you out into the street.
She sat you down on a kitchen stool and tried to bandage
your head with rags she pulled out from under the sink,
after she disinfected the wound with vinegar. You hadn't
cried out, your attention was on her underpants on a clothes-
line that stretched from the door to the window, underpants
that dripped on your aching skull. Underpants as large as
a parachute.

The fluttering of her hands around your head didn't stop her from talking. She didn't doubt your guilt, but accused your father of lacking intelligence. He would have done better to burn your books than to bleed you like a pig. All your troubles came from your studies. They had thwarted your brain by making you write from left to right when your origins indicated the contrary. The fault could be traced back to France, which had imposed its tongue on Arab mouths.

She gave you as an example her own sons and daughters. All lazy do-nothings, thieves, but healthy, with the grace of Allah. "Your Hamidou, Sitt Latifa, pulls his rod out at every street corner, shakes it in the faces of young women, even of old women, lets it piss in the middle of the street, sticks it in the hole of the milkman's mule," *say the malicious gossips.*

You pretend not to have heard.

"Your Abboudi vacillates between two sexes, some others keep telling me. Goat and ram at once, frightened virgin and zebra." *Do they want me to castrate him, when eunuchs are no longer in fashion and no sultan wants them in his harem? What's more, there are no more sultans, no more harems. Abboudi is alive, that's what's essential. They are the spitting image of their father, as depraved as he was, may Allah deepen his Turba. Abou Hamidou had one preoccupation: his cock. He washed it, he powdered it, he aired it out often while the rest of him stank. An incredible thing, he found a way to ejaculate when giving up the ghost. Hanged for having spoken ill of France and its Mandate. The same bad seed goes from generation to generation. But as long as they have their health . . .*

Sitt Latifa sent you home at the first light of dawn: the neighbors mustn't see you at her house.

"As long as I have my health," *you repeated with each step, in a drowsy voice.*

The three girls entrusted to his sister-in-law at the beginning of July barely resembled the ones he took back
at the end of September. My father did not hide his dis-
satisfaction. Three blackamoors burst in on him, with
woodcutters' hands and goats' hooves. Our grown and
widened feet could barely fit into our old shoes. We
had to walk with our toes folded under, carefully. The
house seemed so dark to us after living out of doors,
and the pomegranate tree that bled on the threshold,
obscene. I had had my period for the first time, and the
sight of the bloody liquid nauseated me.

The paternal voice crammed down the fire under the
pots, crammed down the nettles in front of the door,
crammed us down on ourselves. We shrank. To eat or
to sleep at fixed hours was torture to us. In Tantine's
village we had fallen out with clocks and watches. The
sun that faded daily from our faces left behind a pallor
identical to that of the walls and of the lamp that my
father blew out at nightfall. A brutal dive into darkness, a daily descent into hell. We would grope around
in the dark looking for landmarks: a door or a mirror, anything would do. We cried out when our heads
bumped against an obstacle. Mina took advantage of
the situation to use the swear words she had learned
during the summer.

It was at that time that my mother deserted her marriage bed. She shared our room, slept in her son's bed, her nose plunged into his pillow. Far from her husband, she stirred the embers of her grudge, fed it with unpleasant memories, often invented, in which she had the victim's role and he the executioner's.

That time was a turning point at which each of us headed for the open in her own way: my mother by changing her mattress, my two sisters by changing their language. They spoke "chicken," inserting the syllable "biddy" between the syllables of words, cursed their father in his presence without his understanding a word or becoming angry.

"Ibiddy wobiddydobiddy libiddykibiddy tibiddy kibiddylibiddy mibiddy fabiddythabiddyrididdy" (I would like to kill my father) didn't communicate anything disagreeable to him. He let them speak, let me stray from my habitual trajectory—home-school-home—without asking me the reason.

Forty years later, I still ask myself what might have been the reasons that impelled me every day toward that residential neighborhood so far from our own, where palaces lined a street shaded by giant jacarandas. The gates opened before interminable cars. Behind the windowpanes one could distinguish faces haloed with lassitude. Haughty goddesses hid their eyes behind enormous dark glasses. With daggers at their belts, black giants clothed in caftans woven of golden thread bowed down at their passage when the goddesses walked slowly up the steps leading to their dwellings, a miniature poodle in their arms. Men awaited them in bedrooms that I imagined would be red. Their burning mouths must have marked those diaphanous skins like white-hot irons. The desire that I discovered facing their windows made me stagger. My belly throbbed whenever a hand drew the heavy draperies and a chandelier was extinguished. Imagining those dagger-sharp sexes piercing the shaved pubes bent me in two like a sharp pain.

From shadowed patios, cardplayers' voices and laughter reached me. Beringed hands, visible through the foliage, shuffled, dealt, collected queens, kings, jacks, and aces. Hands that were so smooth compared to my mother's, ruined by housework.

I envied them their frivolousness, their poodles, the sound of water splashing in their fountains, that of the wind in the branches of their trees, their artificial laughter, and even their sighs heavy with innuendo.

"I will live in one of these palaces, marry one of these men, it doesn't matter which one, and I'll give orders to their servants."

Vows pronounced in the shade of a jacaranda that dropped its flowers at each breath of wind; vows fulfilled the same evening on a white page. I kept a journal. I wrote in the light of the streetlamp that partially lit up our bedroom, my left hand protecting the words as if my breath could blow them out.

I was part of that world. I was on intimate terms with those men and those women steeped with their own importance, people who put on tuxedoes and long dresses as soon as night fell. I had my place in the Bentleys and Rolls-Royces that took them from cocktails to dinner parties, then to late suppers in those fashionable restaurants of which they tired quickly, yawning before their plates whose contents they contemplated with boredom. My mother was Doña Isabella, the famous model painted so often by Van Dongen; my father, a princely man of seventy endowed with a poodle's brain: Monsieur Gabriel was the delight of a certain kind of press. To a woman journalist who asked him what he would do if the country went Communist and all his wealth was nationalized, he replied without hesitating: "I would go and live with my friend Isabelle."

Doña Isabella survived all her lovers, and died several times before doing so for good, during a night of heavy bombardment. Since she risked being surprised by death improperly attired, she slept fully dressed, in her last days, seated, her red wig lighting up as each shell exploded, her rubies reflecting all the fires.

She requested of the archbishop, her confessor, that she be buried with all her jewels. "It's thanks to these rings, necklaces and bracelets that they'll recognize me, up there." She said up there, but her gaze went downward, toward hell, where she had a good chance of ending her journey.

Weekly death-agonies would take place, preferably on evenings when her son, nephews, nieces, and other heirs were dining in town. They would come running in tuxedos and evening dresses, shoving each other to be first at the dying woman's bedside. Beringed fingers crumpled lace handkerchiefs. Subtly made-up eyes restrained their tears. Only deep sighs and swoons were permitted before the dying woman, who raved on in a soft voice, heaping abuse upon one and then another of her lovers, reproaching them for their coldness or their assiduousness.

The hiccup that shook her from head to feet announced that the end was near. The men prepared obituary notices. In the kitchen, cocks and hens were being slaughtered to feed those who would come from far off. The butler set up the catafalque in the middle of the salon, there where his mistress had had the habit, fifty years earlier, of receiving her bloodthirsty Turkish lover, Djemal Pasha, who governed the country during the First World War, caused the death of two hundred thousand people, wiped out by famine, and hanged as many from the palm trees in the center of Beirut. The traitors who had called France to their aid to deliver them from the Ottoman yoke were spotted at his mistress's dinner parties. He had them arrested when they left, to be sent directly to the Square of the Martyrs. Traitors recognizable by their black ties and patent-leather shoes, which swung in the night of a town center deserted by any passersby.

Doña Isabella's funeral preparations were completed in record time: the candles delivered directly to the kitchen, the Greek Orthodox archbishop and his archimandrite brought in by the great double doors thrown wide open. A sudden turn in events as soon as the prelate intoned "Christos sanesti." The dying woman sat up in her bed, ordered a soft-boiled egg, gobbled it down with her golden spoon, then belched with pleasure as she scanned the crowd with an astonished eye. She had changed her mind. She no longer wanted to die. Would die another time, since God had lent her life. They all returned to their interrupted dinner parties swearing not to let themselves be had again. They would believe in her death when they had seen the tombstone placed over her coffin with their own eyes.

My journal met the same fate as my brother's nocturnal emissions. Used to searching everything, my father discovered my pages. His hand crushing my arm, he dragged me in front of Doña Isabella's gate, and demanded that I introduce him to my servants, to my gardeners, to my new mother, and especially to my new father.

—The one you're not ashamed of, he specified.

His tone, calm at first, grew more heated as he spoke.

—Show him to me, this father of yours. He'll be able to advise me, tell me how to be loved by my own children.

I can still see him, sweating in his uniform that was too warm for the season, his kepi askew on his head, shouting like a maniac. He had bent over as if he wanted to pick up something, then collapsed at the base of the wall. His head buried in his hands, he had sobbed with sobs that were more like barking, like vomiting, tearless, with a noise that made passersby turn around to stare.

—Your mother is right, he kept repeating between fits of coughing. The curse of the monastery will follow me all my life. I ate holy bread, took advantage of the poor monks.

I helped him get up. I dusted off his jacket. He leaned on me to walk back home, turned into an old man in the space of a few hours. That same evening, his face became impenetrable again. The mask he wore once more showed neither the doubt that had stricken him before Doña Isabella's door nor his tears, but only a boundless rancor.

Dry eyes, a dry heart, everything was dry but the

soup he swallowed in great gulps. An ice floe, that table between us, and his icy stare that went right through me, bumped into the wall then came back to him in an echo. All through the meal, I waited for the right moment to throw myself at his feet and swear to never do it again, even if it meant cutting off my own hand when the desire to write came over me. A knee on the ground and two sentences would have relaxed the atmosphere. But I was nailed to my seat. Even mocking Mina noticed and kept her remarks to herself. My mother ought not to have chosen that evening to take out the photograph of her son, which had arrived in the morning mail. It was meant to take the place of a letter, given the signature and the *Love from Paris* inscribed on the other side.

Perched on Victor Hugo's pedestal, my brother imitated the poet's expression in the shade of a chestnut tree. The photo passed from hand to hand, provoking bursts of laughter before finishing its journey in front of the paternal dinner plate. My father clenched his eyes shut, left the table blindly, groped in the dark for his shotgun hanging in the armoire, loaded it, shouldered it, and went out.

From that night on, my father took to hunting down all the dogs and cats in the neighborhood. He meowed or barked to gain their confidence. The gullible ones who were fooled would fall down stiff, with a bullet straight to the head.

Had his children escaped his authority? If that were the case, he would exercise his power over everything that walked on four legs. Their avengers gathered outside our door, though never pointing to it outright. One doesn't openly accuse an officer of the law. First victim: Falstaff, the Contessa's dog. The noise of the street accordion prevented her from hearing the deadly shot. Falstaff, who had dragged himself to her doorstep, expired as she was teaching a lubricious old man the art of embracing his partner with determination.

"Assassins," she howled from her terrace. All assassins: the racetrack brothers, Aunt Rose, Madame Latifa and her five children. Monsieur Alphonse was an assassin as well, even though he never failed to kiss her hand. Assassins and criminals, all the cretins who turned out their lights at eight o'clock precisely, slept at the same time as the hens and woke up when the rooster decided it was the hour. Assassin, in the singular, aimed for the first time at our father: he had every reason to go off the rails. His son had almost raped his daughter. That was hard for a defrocked monk to take.

A wall of silence grew up around us. Shutters closed as we passed by. Even the dogs crossed the street. The Vinikofs kept their distance from us in their own way. They stopped telling us about their expeditions. Only Mademoiselle Renée, become Madame Renée since her marriage, continued to associate with us. Clad in an ermine-bordered dressing gown, she pulled the treasures of her trousseau out one by one, letting them glisten before my eyes before putting them back in their boxes, between two layers of silky tissue paper.

—It's there that Elias has me, every night, she whispered in my ear while she did my hair. She showed me the marriage bed, covered with pink satin, and then her pregnant belly.

—It will be a boy. That's what Elias wants.

—Why? I asked in as small a voice as possible.

—It's good for his pride, she answered, without taking her eyes off her knitting.

She was knitting in point de riz: one stitch on the outside, one on the inside, and the baby's vest grew beneath my wondering eyes.

Ironing followed the knitting. A pile of shirts and trousers waited in a basket. The four brothers had given up the room to the couple in exchange for services. Renée performed them scrupulously. The sweat that streamed down her beautiful face traced large areolas under her armpits, which she dried by lifting her arms up and revealing two tufts of bluish black hair that fascinated me. Is it ironing that makes your hair grow? I wondered at the sight of my own naked armpits.

Renée allowed herself a break before undertaking the most important item: her husband's saroual. The folds that hung between the legs required a swift and adroit stroke of the iron. She turned it around on its hanger, proud of what she had detested a year earlier. Each saroual costs a fortune, she explained. The embroiderers capable of decorating one can be counted on the fingers of one hand. The tarboosh, a sign of decadence to Christians, had become a rare commodity to Renée. Elias ordered his in Egypt. I had thought she was the prisoner of an iron and a washrag: where had she acquired this knowledge?

She seemed happy. Elias didn't beat her, didn't get drunk. A dark cloud crossed her unmoving eyes. She moved quickly, startled, when I pretended to chase it off, and she burst out laughing. Then she spoke up again:

—He's forbidden me to see a doctor. No man besides himself has the right to touch me. The midwife predicts a difficult birth, given how small I am. The child is upside-down: the head above and the feet turned toward the ground.

Seeing me blush, she blamed herself for having indulged in these confidences and chased me off home, after she perfumed me with essence of carnation.

Renée's anxiety was justified six months later. Her labor lasted a day and a night. Her cries came through the walls, the air, the water in the pool, the mass of nettles, and clutched at my heart. Neighborhood women rushed from the kitchen to the bedroom, which were separated by a patio. Large basins full of red-tinted water were spilled at the foot of the pomegranate tree. A fetid odor impregnated our clothes, our pantry. The four brothers attempted to reason with the husband. A doctor would be able to stop the hemorrhage. He kept shaking his head until morning, until the newborn's cry was followed by the neighbor women's wails of lamentation. I ran over, barefoot, in my nightshirt. On the bedroom's threshold, the pride-drunk father showed his son to his family who had come from their southern village. At the crotch of his saroual, a pile of bloody sheets.

Renée's life was extinguished at the moment the streetlight went out. When she was carried to the cemetery by her four brothers, people said that her blood was still flowing inside the coffin, spangling her wedding dress.

You return from Paris on the day after Renée's funeral.
Lacking space in the house, the family received condolence
calls in the courtyard, around the fountain, on chairs
arranged in a circle as if to close in the grief. You walk
through the black-clad crowd without trying to find out
the cause of this gathering. In any case, no one recognizes
you. The skeletal, pallid boy you are now hardly resembles
the one who left the neighborhood a year ago. You give us
several versions of your stay in Paris, and several of your
return. None of them stay close to reality. You've worked
on films and a bit in the theater, even the circus, almost
married a rich heiress, and then worked in radio, in the
department of oriental languages, though you don't know
a single one, not even the maternal Arabic that you de-
spise. You repeat, as if we were deaf, that you had worked
on the radio, but that you had fled French territory, the
internal security services on your tracks, for having dis-
tributed a flyer against French interests in Algeria.

You stop. You try to remember what comes next, and
we do nothing to help you.

—I ran, ran, ran, took the first boat, traveled in the
hold, swabbed down the deck to pay my passage.

—And your poems?

—I'll tell you. I have really suffered. I've been on the
road for more than a month. Not easy to hitchhike here
from Paris. A Greek short-order cook almost raped me, a
Turkish truck driver tried to strangle me. I walked from
Lyons to Marseilles, then turned left . . .

You are exhausted.

—And your poems?

—In Paris, held hostage by the hotel-keeper: he'll give them back to me when I pay my rent. I owe him for three months.

Sweeping away with a wave of her hand the contradictory stories and the lies spun from whole cloth, your mother opens her arms to you, and her pantry, and your bed, but not her purse, not knowing that money and money alone has brought you back home.

Is it the smell of poor Renée's blood that makes her think of yours? Paris has made her son anemic. She takes you to the laboratory. The blood tests confirm her suspicions. Not only do you lack red blood cells, but, something more serious, your blood is poisoned . . .

—Hashish, she guesses.

—More likely heroin.

She only knew cannabis, the principal crop of her village, and she very nearly called the man of science ignorant. She's known them, addicts, half of North Lebanon smokes, it doesn't leave them in such a state.

—Hashish, that's crap compared to heroin. He-ro-in, he repeats, annoyed.

And she's speechless. She asks for the bill with gestures. Your mother's Calvary began at the door of that laboratory; a quarter of a century long, it would end with her death.

She locks herself up with you when the detoxification cure is over, which was paid for with our household money and turned us into vegetarians. The key is turned in the lock to keep you from finding other addicts. You call her a jailer, an executioner, a cop. She does not protest. She only loses her restraint when you accuse her of not loving you.

Your father keeps his distance, doesn't get involved in your discussions, which go perpetually around in circles. A serpent that bites its own tail. He waits for his moment and stares without seeing at the zombie you have become. He moves away, flattens himself against the wall so as not to brush against you when your paths cross.

Your first outing, a month later, to see your pals at La Palette, lasts until dawn. Standing in the street, your mother watches for you as if that position could hasten your return. Midnight shrinks her into herself. From far off, one would mistake her for some piece of clothing fallen on the ground. The first hours of the morning plunge her head between her knees. Her legs have trouble holding her up, she sits down on the curb. A car stops beside her just when she has given up all hope of seeing you again. Some scruffy boys push you out of the vehicle, then go off in a cloud of dust.

Your feet trace parallel furrows in the gravel as she drags you toward the house. She hides you behind a screen: your father mustn't see your wild-eyed expression, your trembling limbs, nor the blue, green, yellow marks on your forearms. She works at the sewing machine so he won't hear the chattering of your teeth, expostulates about the heat in the middle of December to explain the sweats that soak you from head to feet, speaks loudly, sings, to drown out your voice demanding a fix, a tiny fix, moves the furniture, changes the placement of couches and beds, makes a racket when you howl like a lunatic.

You demand your fix from someone who doesn't know what a fix is; you would be capable of killing her and killing yourself afterwards. The savory dishes she prepares for you with love are trampled underfoot and your mother's heart bleeds at the waste.

—*I didn't ask to eat. Food is for idiots who stuff them-selves, shit, stuff themselves to shit more. What I want can be said in one word: high.*

Before her troubled gaze, you specify: " *To go far away, get really high, above everything.*" You explain to her a hundred times the benefits resulting from a fix, a dose, even minuscule, a hundred times she shakes her head. You propose sharing it with her. You're ready to give her half.

"*And then two of us will take off.*"

She has trouble believing you. One would have to be mad to think that a pinch of powder could turn you into a bird or an angel.

—*But I am an angel. Every suffering being is.*

You write down an address on a scrap of paper, under it you write a name, someone you trust. You give it to her, feverish, kiss her hands as if she were a bishop. Sus-picious, she pulls them back, hides them behind her back, then sits on them.

—*Are you my mother or shit! Prove that you love me!*

She proves it with that mouth twisted in despair. She no longer knows how to cry.

More and more violent demands during the night. Your father, who can't sleep, leaves the house unobtrusively to telephone from the grocery. He calls the asylum and claims that a madman is terrorizing his family.

Two giants in white coats break into the house and carry you out to the ambulance, which is waiting with all its lights out under poor Renée's window. You continue to struggle. You turn toward your father just before the am-bulance doors close on you, you call on him for help:

—*Tell them, Papa, that I'm not crazy!*

The word Papa makes him flee. He begins to run in the opposite direction from the ambulance. Your mother *grabs her broom, sweeps inside and then outside to erase any trace of footsteps. The noise of the broom on the ground covers the sound of her weeping.*

I write my first poem, the same night, with your pen, on the page that you hadn't been able to fill. The poet died the day he met the powder. Poem written for you, against you. I showed it to you later, during a visit to the asylum. Your face darkened.

—Your father will have you locked up if he finds out.

You warned me, not at all envious. You saved your anger for your mother, who held a bag of sweets out to you.

—I need my freedom, not candy. You betrayed me. You plotted with your cop to lock me up. You think you can make everything all right with your tears. What are you waiting for, to burst out crying?

She sniffles, restrains herself. Her attention shifts to your mouth. There is a tooth missing.

—They pulled your tooth?

—A poor kid. He took my mouth for a fly and swatted it.

—And this? she went on, continuing her inventory down to a blood-streaked knee.

—A human bite. Your son sleeps in the same ward as twenty nutcases.

You warned her. You would get out by your own means if she attempted nothing by hers. She pointed out the walls, the countless security doors, the bolted gates. Nothing could discourage you.

In the bus that took us back home, she uttered this sentence:

—We'll take your brother back home if, by some misfortune, your father should have an accident.

Hell, as described in our catechism, was at home with us, within our walls sealed off by nettles. Arguments burst out like storms. Blame and reproaches, from both sides, washed through, a muddy water that splattered everything. We were no longer in the era when my mother muttered her discontent in a low voice. She declaimed it now. The curse of the monastery became part of every discussion. She enumerated our past troubles and those that were to come. Our father was out of work, and as for us, we were old maids: no one would marry us, given our brother's reputation.

—They'll always be on your hands. Do you hear me?

He couldn't hear her. His hands glued to his ears kept him sheltered from maternal predictions.

She avenged herself for her years of submission, and he riposted with silences that could last for weeks, for months. Had he been cleverer, he would have reminded her that the curse foretold for him exactly such a marriage, with a woman as gloomy and arid as he was himself.

Austere to the point of asceticism, so sober they were frugal, abstinent to the point of complete renunciation, our parents had only disdain for verbal outpourings, and considered life itself a kind of Calvary.

The Christian part of town was celebrating Palm Sunday. The odor of candles suffused the air. Voices from the landing had drawn me out of bed. My mother was talking with a woman dressed in a long black cloak. One of those fortune-tellers who go from house to house begging, if not outright pilfering. My mother insisted that she had no need to know her future and was pushing the annoying visitor away with decisive movements. Their intonations presaged a fight. Threats were uttered on one side and the other. My appearance, barefoot, in a nightgown, calmed my mother down. But the Bedouin didn't take her eyes off me.

—That girl, she said, will live in three countries, will marry three men, and speak three languages. She will shut the third one up in books.

What more might she have said, if my mother, scandalized at the idea that I would be married three times, had not driven her away?

Three years ago, when my mother was dying, I recalled to her the anger and the violence with which she had sent the Bedouin woman about her business. I wanted, with these memories, to prevent her from slipping into a coma, to delay her death.

The same anger pierced through her stare. She admitted to me that she had never been able to forget those dire predictions, especially after my divorce, then after my widowhood; she was obsessed by my failures and my inability to hold onto my husbands. She looked for the woman, who was often seen in the neighborhood, extended her search to the nomads' tents pitched on a vacant lot outside of town. No one knew her. That witch with a face covered with tattoos: had she come up out of the nettles that surrounded the house, or from the pomegranate tree that was reborn, yearly, from its dried-out stump?

By that third language, shut up in books, was the fortune-teller alluding to the poetry I had stolen from my brother? Thefts committed in the night, when the city was asleep, behind the back of fate and of the father who had convinced us that poetry was an accursed genre that spread madness. I wrote in darkness, my eyes closed so as not to lose a single word.

Pages that were illegible in the morning: the letters clambered over each other, seemed to seethe out of an anthill.

Macha and Yara Vinikof called my writings cabalistic. The devil was using me to send a message to their father about the treasure, or even perhaps to my brother, locked up for months now with the madmen.

—You ought to listen to him, said Yara. Perhaps he's trying to give you advice.

—You're wrong not to take him seriously, continued Macha. Devils are like men, there are bad ones, good ones, even virtuous ones. Everything depends on the way they were sent to Hell.

She paused before uttering this last sentence:

—Your mother ought to go and see the magus Garabed. He could cure your brother. Your father put a spell on him.

*One day is the same as the next one for your mother, lost
and distraught between her pots and pans and her iron.
She lets your visiting day go by, and then remembers it
while doing the dishes. Two plates drop from her hands.
Taken over by rage, she throws a third one after them.
She leaves the shards on the ground, takes her place in the
doorway, stares unseeingly at the nettles manhandled by
the wind. A storm is brewing. Bolts of lightning stripe the
sky above the pond. The sky and your mother's eyes hold
back their tears. Only torrential rains would bring some
peace to her heart.*

*You appear at the end of the path at the moment when
the rumbling breaks out, rattling doors and windows.
Barefoot, in tattered pajamas, you don't dare come closer.
Your clothing streams with water. Mama gets up, runs to
meet you, brings you into the house, kneels down in front
of you, sponges the blood running down your lacerated
heels. To her panic, you reply, "It's nothing." You had
waited for nightfall to scale the wall, a wall with broken
glass along its top.*

*It's nothing, since here you are together and she is tak-
ing care of you, in front of your father who watches the
scene with his predator's eye. He's waiting for the pro-
pitious moment to go and turn you in. She has guessed
this and has barred the door to him with her outstretched
arms. She forbids him to go out, and he bows to his wife's
will for the first time.*

*"It's nothing." Two words rolled like pebbles in the
river. You rely on their sonority. "It's nothing" was the*

diagnosis of the male nurse when you showed him your broken tooth, then your knee bitten down to the bone. A dog bite, he reported, despite the marks of human teeth and the absence of any dog in the asylum. Your mother is taking care of your body once more, washing it, feeding it, disinfecting the wounds, and forgetting the essential: an envelope with the letterhead of a Parisian publisher with a postmark from the seventh arrondissement. She gave it back to you at the last minute, when the orderlies, the same ones as the first time, burst into the house to carry you away, half asleep, in the same ambulance. A letter that sows discord in the family. For years, we asked ourselves what had become of it. What was in it? And how had you lost it during your journey? A turbulent journey: you kept trying to escape despite the padlocked doors and the straitjacket that bound your limbs.

A journalist who was investigating your past gave it back to me, six years ago. "A souvenir of your brother," he said to me. How had he gotten hold of it? He said he had found it in your files. No one had opened it. Civil war had slackened the attention of the people in charge: he had passed a whole day at the asylum, intent on your case history. You had been subjected to excessive electroshock treatments after your escape. They had to prevent you from trying again.

I have never opened that letter. A rejection from the publisher would have made me doubt your gifts as a poet. And in the opposite case, I'd have died of remorse.

A brutal winter tore the drainpipes from the walls, made the pond overflow, and turned the courtyard into a swamp where brackish water stagnated. The buildings' façades, covered with mold, were green, red, and gray. The five houses, with their laundry rooms and garrets, looked like a toothless mouth. They seemed to push and crowd against each other, to press their walls together to drive out the inhabitants. Renée, Falstaff, my brother. Of the three who had disappeared, the Contessa's dog was the one most visibly mourned. The Contessa closed her door to prospective dancers and her heart to music; her sobs replaced the tango. Only a miracle could revive stones and people struck with the same curse. This miracle happened at our landlady's house. The image of the Holy Virgin wept on Aunt Rose's wall. Her cries brought out the neighbors, who told everyone in the district. There was no doubt about it: the holy picture was weeping. She wept for the stupid death of poor Renée, the unjust death of Falstaff, and the forced departure of my brother to the madhouse.

Impelled by curiosity or by faith, the inhabitants of the lower town rushed into our courtyard, waded through our mud, lit candles on the rim of the pond, muttered prayers in Arabic, in Syrian, in Aramaic, in Hebrew, crossed themselves with three of five fingers. To place your hand on the Holy Face cost fifty piastres, a hundred to wipe the glass covering the picture with your handkerchief. The crippled were hoisted on the shoulders of those who were not. A formidable wave of solidarity brought together people who came from different religions and classes. The odor of melted candle wax mingled with that of grilled lamb brochettes sold by Madame Latifa, her face flushed from blowing on the coals.

Calm returned at nightfall. The unaccustomed silence drew me toward the pond, over which I leaned in contemplation of the reflected clouds that hung above it. Sometimes, from between two cottony masses, Renée loomed up in her wedding dress. The water's rippling made her sway. One might have thought she was dancing. Her transparence was becoming to her corpse's complexion. Her mouth opened and closed like a fish's. She asked me for news about her baby, and I didn't know what to answer. Her brothers must have been looking after him. Their shutters, closed in mourning, let no noise pass through.

Renée and my brother, born in the same year, left the neighborhood at the same time, but for different destinations. The silence that crushed the young woman dead in childbirth was as terrible as the deafening noise that he alone could hear within his head.

You come toward us wavering and zigzagging. A sailboat that has lost its mast. Your feet go in different directions as if your two legs belonged to two different bodies.

Wednesday. Visiting day. The head doctor makes sure to meet your mother first to prepare her for the violent change you have undergone. The treatment is taking its course in progressive stages. It was necessary, after your second attempt to escape.

—One, she says.

—Two, the psychiatrist insists. He went over the wall again three days ago. Looking for an Englishwoman painter, an eccentric, who left the country more than a year ago. The neighbors called the police; he was beating on her door and howling "Open up, Sylvia! Open the door for Rimbaud!"

The same sentence all night long. He shouted, he was threatening to break everything. He was convinced that she was there. Inside.

The orderlies brought back a rag. He was sobbing like a child, his clothes were wet with tears and mucus: he didn't even wipe his eyes. I decided to double the dose. It was necessary.

—Dose? she says, dumbfounded. She had heard the same word from your lips. Is it possible that the psychiatrist himself gives it to his patients?

She finds the strength to rise, to hide her disappointment. Her hands grip her fake-crocodile purse, as if she were afraid he would rip it away from her. She takes her leave of him with a brief nod of her head, without un-

clenching her teeth, and moves away in a dignified manner toward the visitors' room where you are waiting for her.

You brush away her hand as it traces the sign of the cross on your forehead. The cotton soaked with the tears of the miraculous Virgin remains gripped between her fingers. Your attention goes instead to the bag of sweets you had refused during the last visit. You rip off the wrappers and cram three candies at once into your mouth: pink, red, white. You keep on putting together the same assortment, the three colors probably have a special meaning for you. You answer her questions sullenly when your mouth is not too full to permit it. Yes, you are happy here. Charming neighbors, helpful and obliging porters. You think you are in a summer camp, perhaps at a seaside resort. "Hello, old chap!" "Hello, old chap!" You have many friends. The tap on the shoulder given to you by a giant with a shaved head shakes you from head to foot. You cough, choke, spit out the mixed debris of white, pink, and red.

To your indignant mother, you explain that he's a friend of yours.

—He loughed me up fol a joke.

The letter R disappeared from that moment on. You ask for "olanges," a "wool scalf," a new "led shilt." You have acquired a Chinese accent without ever going to China. Once the bag of sweets is empty, you turn your back on us. You turn around before being swallowed up by a door and tell your mother not to be too sad about the weeping Virgin. In the end she'll get over the death of her son.

Red, pink, white, I repeat to myself while going through the three security chambers, then the reinforced door. Candies the colors of your life. Rose-colored, as you would have wished it. White, the color of the powder that erased the hostile world and replaced it with another one whose vague contours seemed sweet and soft. Red because of that neighbor who had seen you in the Place de l'Étoile in Paris, a year earlier. You were putting your foot in front of every car that came by, and then pulling it back at the last possible moment, just as the wheel brushed it. You were bullfighting with the machine, you were measuring yourself against steel, with, in your ears, the applause of an imaginary crowd.

My brother was wrong when he claimed that the Virgin would get over her sorrow. Her tears continue to moisten the glass beneath the stunned gazes of the believers and the more suspicious ones of the reporters.

The press has established its headquarters in our neighborhood. There is even talk of a visit from His Holiness the Pope. The journalists interview the talkative, photograph the taciturn in the shadow of the pomegranate tree, or leaning on the rim of the pool. Our sufferings provide an ideal ground for paranormal phenomena. Georges Vinikof has been chasing demons for years, pursuing them with a pickaxe from the seashore to the innermost countryside. The four racetrack brothers bet on the races out of necessity, to raise their orphan nephew. A mother dead in childbirth and a father in prison. The widower protests in vain that he is right there, no one listens to him. It's not for his saroual or his tarbouche that they'll spoil their picture. The former convict would do well to make himself scarce. It's bad form to interrupt a broadcast, and especially to interpose oneself between the camera and a child.

The Contessa doesn't need to explain herself. The state of disarray of her apartment and of her person express themselves with no commentary. The chignon coming undone in wisps, the circles around her eyes, are signs of great suffering. She mumbles in a groggy voice that after Falstaff's death, life is insupportable to her, without mentioning that Falstaff was a dog. She who used to teach worldly people to dance staggers when she stands up. She no longer knows how to walk.

We cut ourselves the lion's share with a father who is a defrocked monk, distinguished servant of France and its Mandate, personal interpreter for General de Gaulle during his tour of the Middle East. We exhibit a medal with the image of the great man, a so-called gift of the general to our progenitor. No one is in a position to verify this. Many are suffering from migraines. The odor of Madame Latifa's mechoui distorts judgment, and nauseates everyone, particularly the foreign journalists.

We are careful not to mention you. Unlike the sick, who attract compassion, the mad provoke a feeling of unease.

Only your mother continues to visit you. Faithful to your Wednesdays, she goes without thinking or asking herself whether she is doing it from habit or out of real need, yours or her own. I content myself with the information she gives me, whose explanations I look for in the dictionary. She says electroshock, and I see your head confined in a helmet attached to wires: the current grooves into your neurons and makes them ring like bells to rid them of their troubled waters.

Your mistreated child's fears, your adolescent anguish, your man's desires are jostled together in a hellish din. Once the session is over, an apocalyptic silence fills your skull. Five continents and as many oceans all struck dumb. The emptiness behind your pallid face, the void in your eyes sewed shut with threads of fire. You sleep twenty-four hours at a stretch.

To your mother, who goes into raptures at your capacity to sleep, you say that there's a bit of death in sleep, just enough to be able to wake up.

—But you look incredibly well, she answers.

—The dead have smooth features, and relaxed faces.

She doesn't understand what the dead have to do with the two of you. You confuse her, and she tires you by her slowness of understanding. You are eager to see her leave, once she has taken your dirty laundry and given you the delicacies she bought with the housekeeping money. She deprives us of what we need to satisfy your desire for the unnecessary: Nestlé's chocolate bars, English biscuits, and the famous red, pink, and white candies. Knowing that you're content with this tiny life takes away any desire I have to see you. Wednesday is once again a day like any other for me. I went to the asylum when I knew you were burning with desire to escape. The electroshock sessions and the neuroleptic drugs have cropped your wings. You are a fallen angel, an amputated bird.

The tears of the Virgin who wept on our landlady's wall changed the behavior of the five houses' inhabitants. The interviews they gave hither and yon gave them the habit of lying. Everyone lied in his own way, and according to his means. From that time on, they began their sentences with "Before the tears," or "After the tears began." The lachrymal secretions of the Mother of God played a historical role in their personal calendars. Before the tears, I rarely lied. After the tears, I took to lying regularly and diligently. At home, I explained my absences in the evening by saying I had been doing research at the library; elsewhere I stated that my father was a general, my mother a medical doctor, and my brother, an attaché at the embassy in Paris. I was in a false position everywhere, except within myself, where I was convinced I was telling the truth. And because a never-pruned pomegranate tree darkened the rooms we lived in, I searched out artificial lights, spotlights, photographers' false daylight. I entered all the beauty contests, in the city, in the suburbs, the location didn't matter. I was crowned *Miss Agriculture,* although I couldn't tell a cow from a bull; *Miss Sport,* although if I jumped ten inches I'd tangle my feet in the jump rope; *Miss Travel,* although I had never crossed the borders of the country. I strutted in a bathing suit across the stages, swaying so as to best show off breasts, legs, buttocks, which would hoist me above my station. I became the daughter of the general and the doctor when the photographers kneeling at my feet asked me to look at the camera.

Bitter awakenings, the next morning, facing the field of nettles, to the odor of gas coming from the kitchen, to the sound of the pot under which my mother was trying to light a fire.

The people who brought me home at the end of an evening would leave me in front of another door. My choice was always the most majestic. News of my triumphs arrived at my father's ears, and earned me a private discussion behind closed doors. I denied everything, despite my photograph in the newspaper. The girl with the banner *Miss Summer* across her chest looked like me, nothing more, and it was only by chance that we also had the same name.

—And that? he said, his finger pointing at the minuscule bit of fabric that served as my garment.

I expected his anger, not this comment made in a tone of desperation.

—The neighbors will take me for a miser, not willing to pay for a yard of cloth to cover his daughter's body.

Had the idea of putting me out of the house like my brother crossed his mind? He did nothing of the sort. A girl thrown out on the street would turn out badly.

Returning from one of those evenings, during which I had been crowned *Miss Andean Mountain Range,* I found the whole neighborhood in a commotion. A miracle had taken place, a resurrection.

—Exactly like Lazarus, the grocer, a man known for his fine salads and his bad character, explained to me.

—Mademoiselle Renée, I pronounced in a trembling voice.

He looked daggers at me.

It was Falstaff, come back from the beyond on foot. He had scratched at his mistress's door, then barked when she was slow to open it. The poor woman cried out to anyone who'd listen that it was a miracle. It really was Falstaff, and not a distant cousin or a brother, a common enough phenomenon among canines, and among the Chinese as well, according to Monsieur Alphonse.

Life took up where it had left off at the Universal Institute, but with tangos interspersed with tender murmurings.

"My angel, mi amor, Mama's amor"—this did not please my father, who tolerated no laxity with the French language. Would he relapse into crime because of mongrel vocabulary, and kill Falstaff two, whom his mother took for Falstaff one?

With fine aim, the Contessa asked to meet with him, and led him to understand that she would be honored if he would agree to carry her doggy to the baptismal font.

—You will be his godfather. You will watch over him like his own papa.

And of course he accepted. From the next morning on, he took up walking the resuscitated one on his leash, to do his business. A leash studded with diamonds, swore the ignorant, who had never seen jewels of paste. Their two silhouettes ambling alongside the gutter at nightfall moved the passersby. So fine to see, the proud soldier with a star on his shoulder and his freshly groomed companion.

I cast a shadow over my two sisters. They swore they had not grown a quarter of an inch since I had been taking myself for Marilyn Monroe. Accursed family. As in the forest, where the tall trees asphyxiate the shorter ones, we smothered each other, we crushed each other.

A squeezing down from on high. Had I not written my first poem the very day my brother stopped writing?

Many, in the neighborhood, accused the Virgin of favoritism. My father, touched more generously by her grace than the racetrack brothers or Monsieur Alphonse, or even Aunt Rose, though it was she who sheltered the Virgin on her wall, became tolerant, good, affectionate. His love for humanity knew no bounds. He took to loving everyone, with the exception of blacks, beggars, and his own son. One could read on his face his respect for those smaller than he, for those weaker than he, but not for those who were poorer.

    —My eldest daughter will be elected *Miss Universe*.

    An unthinkable proposition a month earlier. My narcissism became so acute that I wanted to look at my image in anything that could reflect it: shop-fronts, windowpanes, puddles in the gutter.

I often had the same nightmare. I was living in a dark house at the edge of a forest. I would go from room to room in search of a mirror in which to capture my reflection: the crowd that surrounded the property would condemn me to death if I returned empty-handed. I ran from room to room in the hope of finding a reflecting glass, but none of the rooms held one. The night became blacker, I bumped against the walls, against the locked doors; I cried out in pain. My own screams woke me.

"My daughter will be elected *Miss Universe*." My father had announced it to everyone in the neighborhood while walking Falstaff. The man whose death I had wished for morning, noon, and night had become the ally of my megalomania, the accomplice of my delusions. I began to love him, to fear for his life. The house suddenly seemed larger to me, the field of nettles was touching, and, incredibly, the moon, which our one mirror had never reflected, appeared in it nightly at a regular time.

Miss Universe, a title that would reflect on the inhabitants of all five houses. To thank my father for his courtesies to Falstaff, the Contessa ought to teach me to walk gracefully, and particularly, to dance.

—You'll send her to me tomorrow.

A generous offer made through the iron grill where every evening my father brought back to his mistress a dog exhausted by his walk. Falstaff had become attached to my father. He preferred to piss on his boots rather than move away from him, and my father, softened, wiped them with his pocket handkerchief.

Clasped in the arms of a portly man in his fifties, I moved up and down the Contessa's drawing room under the gaze of Falstaff, instructed to bite the calves of those who trod on their partners' feet. My own dance partner's sweat fell between my breasts, from whence it dripped down to my navel. Five steps forward, five steps back, and through the semi-transparent curtains, my father's illuminated face tracked my every movement, turned with the music and the sun. From the place where he was standing, he had a view of the dancers' heads, not of their knees, those of my partner digging into my crotch in alternation.

The man exasperated me: his mustache smelled of grilled lamb. I detested those arms that gripped me, that breath on my neck, that vacuous toad face, but I tolerated those knees that were making me discover sensations that increased until a wave of pleasure broke over me and made me grab onto him so as not to stumble. The music and my heart stopped at the same time. The harsh cry that broke from my throat coincided with the crash of cymbals announcing the end of the tango.

Terrifying pleasure. My legs were like cotton, and in my throat a taste of melted lead. The word perdition so dear to my father. I was losing my soul in deviating from the line of conduct I had drawn for myself to succeed, conduct that consisted of charming others but giving nothing of myself. The example of my brother, enslaved to his senses, was there to serve as a warning. I was convinced that only the affluent could permit themselves to be depraved.

The image of four women, three young and one old, whom I had seen in a shop in the center of town, was fixed in my memory. Faces outrageously made-up, hair bleached blond, the three younger ones were trying on dresses while observed by the older one, who was paying. The youngest, almost a child, incessantly wiped the saliva dripping from her mouth. She stripped naked quite naturally, showing a shaven pubis.

—If it isn't sad to see that! exclaimed the saleswoman, as soon as they had turned their backs to leave.

I followed them with my eyes as far as that dark little street where they disappeared into a building covered with neon signs. I learned that day that the town's brothels were restricted to that district. Leaning over the wrought-iron balconies, the prostitutes called out to the passersby, enticing them with their breasts, which they exhibited on the railing. The same gesture as the greengrocer showing his fruit. My brother had told me about it, but I hadn't believed him.

Long held in check, the hostility between the Lebanese and the Palestinian refugees finally bursts into violence. The city is boiling like a kettle. The center of town has been bombed. When your mother comes to reassure you, you ask her for news of the brothels' neighborhood, not of ours.

Your question embarrasses her. She has never had a thought for those women who spend their days in bed, even when they are working. For her, beds are reserved for sleep and sickness.

—Tell Marika the Greek that I'm worried about her.

She suppresses a visible start, then asks you how much you used to pay that creature.

—Pay, pay, that's the only word you're capable of saying. But what do you know about affection?

—What were you doing in those people's houses? she asks in a tight-lipped voice.

—We would talk. I'd read my poems to Marika, and she would listen. Whole afternoons stretched out between two sheets.

—And why not sitting in the parlor?

—Wasn't any, you say in a feeble voice, and your lovely lucidity has only lasted the space of three sentences. "Wasn't any, wasn't any" your lips repeat, no longer knowing what they say. You hold the sentence open like an umbrella. You go off into fantasy again. You need a compass, so as not to get lost at night when you go to the toilet; you need shoes with spiked soles to climb the mountains that surge up in your dreams; you need a soundproof jacket to protect you from evil waves.

She acquiesces, refuses none of your demands, which she will forget as soon as she goes through the great gateway.

Your compass, your hiking shoes seemed fantastic at first hearing, but you explained them in this text written before you left for Paris, which I found between two pages of the dictionary:

—Thus, it came about one night that my brother left the house without my knowledge. You can imagine my fury when, the next morning, at the break of day, I went to open the door to him.

—So then, you don't give a fig for me? I said to him.

My brother did not answer. He let slip to the floor a sack filled with carpenter's tools, and led me to the window.

—Look what I've done! he said, directing my gaze to the mountain.

I thought I was dreaming.

From the summit to the base, the mountain had been completely transformed into giant armchairs and tables of elaborate style.

My joy knew no bounds. I opened my arms to my brother to congratulate him. However, another spectacle was being prepared at the other side of the mountain. In the time it took for us to break from our embrace, we saw, to our great astonishment, an unusual mass of clouds metamorphose into men and women of all ages, who descended to take their places in that enormous open-air casino.

Waiter-clouds appeared and served them cocktails. Others brought ice cream and coffee, or distributed playing cards.

The first group gave themselves over completely to their play. They toasted each other, gambled and swore to their hearts' content. Some, more romantic, paid court to girl-clouds, daring to place from time to time a discreet kiss on a shoulder.

And when the pleasure party finished, these strange revelers paid their bill and departed as they had come.

We're far from your first poems, which you claimed to be writing under the dictation of Victor Hugo, who had chosen you among all the living to complete his posthumous works. No lyricism, not the slightest trace of emotion. Hugo had taken back from you the flame that he had confided to you in a moment of wild generosity. He was angry with you since you had committed the sacrilege of being photographed on the base of his statue.

The parish priest came to visit us during the week following my initiation to the tango. The bouquet of red roses that advanced behind him hid my despised partner. My mother did not understand the cause of my pallor, nor my haste to shut myself up behind a door. The visit lasted ten minutes.

Her face, when she came to find me, was lit up with joy. The gentleman with the bouquet actually wanted to marry me, despite my reputation. A single dance at the Contessa's had sufficed to convince him that I was the wife he required. He alone could calm my frenzy for rushing to wealthy suburbs and balls. Only a man of his sort, in his fifties, would know how to tame me. My mother used her fingers to enumerate to me the benefits that would accrue to me from this union.

—You'll live in a real apartment. You'll be driven in a car by a liveried chauffeur. You'll have plenty of money

She lowered her voice a notch to add what followed:

—You'll give a little to your mother.

Then, as if as an excuse:

—It will be for your poor brother.

She stopped. Her tongue had outstripped her thoughts. I bore her no grudge. I was even ready to follow her sense of things: to emerge from my hiding place, to take the hand of the man who inspired me with nothing but disgust, but my father's voice stopped me in my tracks.

—Better not to bring up this subject with my daughter. To talk to her of marriage might disturb her. She's still a child . . .

Should this answer be credited to the Virgin who had taken up residence on Aunt Rose's wall?

The liquid that had wet the holy picture during a whole season stopped abruptly. The Virgin no longer wept. The source of her tears had dried up. The reporters and the visitors came up against a closed door. Word-to-mouth gossip traveled quickly. No one came any longer to kneel there. No one came to light the least candle, nor to put the smallest coin in the collection box at the door. The courtyard was abandoned to empty beer cans, sandwich and candy wrappers left by the believers, to film cartons thrown away by the photographers. No one asked for news of our landlady. We had trouble recognizing her when she appeared on her doorstep after ten days' absence. She was a shadow of herself. You thought you were seeing her profile when you looked at her straight on. Her emaciated face resembled a quarter-moon. The doctor, an Armenian Communist chosen for his low fees and not his competence, advised her to see an ophthalmologist because you'd have to be blind to think that cardboard could weep.

She went to the hospital for a consultation when her left eye had taken on a permanent squint and the left corner of her mouth drooped down to her shoulder. The diagnosis left her no hope. She had three months to live. A tumor as big as the pomegranates that ripened in front of our doorway was growing inside her skull. The comparison was not gratuitous; the oncologist was well aware of our suffering at the sight of that juicy fruit that our landlady forbade us to pick, fruit that made our mouths water when it burst with a dry noise, disclosing red seeds full of nectar.

She seemed annihilated and really dumbfounded,

not remembering very well if the doctor had given her three months or three weeks to live. My father was unanimously designated to go for more information: he was the only one among the adult tenants able to sign his name, the only one who spoke French.

We waited for his return. Everyone in the neighborhood kept watch for his silhouette, which could be distinguished from anyone else's because of his peaked military cap and the single star shining on his epaulette.

To our questions, he answered repeatedly, "You will soon know everything." He wiped his forehead several times with his handkerchief, asked for a lemonade, then retired to the toilet where we could hear him puffing and panting—a woman in childbirth couldn't have done better. Re-emerged among us after having meticulously soaped his hands, he drew out of his pocket a scroll so long it could have been a sultan's edicts. The paper unrolled, he cleared his throat, and looked over the assembled listeners to make sure no one was missing.

It was in absolute reverence that we listened to his reading of the information given by the oncologist, and recorded by himself.

"The radiological examination not having provided satisfactory results, we proceeded with a sterotaxic examination, which permitted access via a closed skull, by means of a punctiform opening, to an intracerebral target defined to the nearest millimeter, via three-dimensional imaging, in order to situate the affected area . . ."

And so on for forty minutes.

This long and arduous recitation did us no good at all. To the Contessa, who requested that he abbreviate it, he replied that science was not reducible. To the afflicted woman, who made him understand that she would be infinitely grateful if he could explain it in simpler terms, he riposted that it would be an insult to medical science to vulgarize it. Knowing his immoderate love for France and its language, Madame Latifa should not have dared to ask for a translation into Arabic.

—Never! he barked. The language of assassins, of Bedouins, of chicken thieves and kidnappers.

Poor Aunt Rose! As if a slantwise mouth and crossed eyes weren't enough misfortune, her illness made her senile. The harpy we were accustomed to who claimed her rent in a surly tone, now made the rounds of her tenants and gave them each the sum she ought to have collected. The world upside-down. The unscrupulous pocketed it without asking for explanations. Appalled, my father argued with the poor woman till he was exhausted, gave her back all the money, which she put back by force into his own pocket, but which he then crammed into her bra. They could have continued like this till the end of time if the racetrack brothers had not had a brilliant idea. They seized the object in dispute. They would bet it on the races. Sea Eagle had a good chance of winning the daily double.

That same evening, I saw Renée again in the water of the pool. A sign of great distress, she clung close to the bottom. With an accusing finger, she pointed out to me the house that had been hers. Was it about her baby or her brothers that she was uneasy? She had no reason to trouble herself about the former. His uncles took care of him with an unimaginable devotion. They sterilized his bottles, mixed up his vegetable purees, took him out for a walk every afternoon in his pram, then put him to sleep to the sound of the same lullaby that they sang to him in chorus without knowing to what language it belonged. The words came from French, the intonations from Italian: *"Anagrosocoqaptitsovernapaso"*

They would chant it for hours. Where had they learned it? It took me years to decipher it. One had to separate the syllables to get: Ane a gros os, coq a petits os, ver n'a pas d'os (Donkey has big bones, rooster has little bones, worm has no bones).

The four old bachelors chanted "Anagroso" while the baby's father twiddled his thumbs in a cell. They had so often repeated to him that he would end up in prison that he had finally committed an indiscretion.

No one sang "Anagroso" the following Sunday. A funereal silence covered their house. The rooms plunged in darkness, the howls of the baby whom no one had the will to console found their explanation in perusal

of the racing papers. Sea Eagle had come in last. All of
Aunt Rose's rent money had gone up in smoke. One
more trial that took away the scrap of sense remaining
to her.

Disgusted with hospitals and hippodromes, Aunt Rose turned to hypnotists, bonesetters, magicians. A healer who lived in a pigeon house in the old town questioned her at length on her habits. It was in these that he would find the sources of the illness that was wearing her down.

Did she sleep on her left side or her right? Did she write with her left hand or her right, bent over or sitting erect? When she got out of bed in the morning, did she first put her right foot or her left foot on the floor, and her rooster, did he crow with his head turned to the left or to the right?

—I don't know, I don't remember, she answered to each question.

She wrote neither bent over nor sitting erect: she was illiterate.

She left with a mirror attached to her skull, which was meant to attract the illness to itself, drink in its reflection, and then break itself into a thousand fragments once it had guzzled the bad blood within her down to the last drop. Another healer, a Yemenite, relieved her of her last piastres after having prescribed the application of tobacco leaves soaked in vinegar. She walked around for a week with a reddish brown yarmulke plastered to her head. The liquid that dripped from it traced red rivulets on her cheeks and gave her a vague resemblance to the Christ.

The unfortunate woman, she became poorer and

poorer as treatment after treatment proved ineffective and the tumor grew.

She began to repeat herself endlessly, and asked the four racetrack brothers ten times a day for news of Sea Eagle.

—He's very well, thanks, they replied, without daring to look her in the face.

Hospitalized when she could no longer recognize anyone, she was operated on by a surgeon who had the singular reputation of taking flight at the sight of blood. For Aunt Rose, there was no bleeding, nor the slightest post-operative complication. All went well, and the pain that drilled through the sick woman's skull was described as incomprehensible and abnormal until the day the surgical nurse complained of the loss of his scissors. The X ray found them stuck between the pituitary gland and the hypothalamus. Re-operating was unthinkable, given the patient's state of indigence. She was sent home on the bus.

Aunt Rose was as dilapidated as the houses she rented out. From her sloppily sutured skull oozed a liquid that stained the sheets and pillowcases. It emitted a nause-ating odor. The Armenian doctor, with whom she con-tinued to have hostile relations, blamed this discharge on the Yemenite charlatan. The blindness with which she was afflicted could be imputed, according to him, to the first healer. Instead of capturing the illness than was sapping her strength, the mirror had seized the light of her eyes, had sucked the juice of her retinas and chewed on her corneas like vulgar chewing gum. These were his own words. No one dared contradict him.

She took a week to die, seven times longer than

Mademoiselle Renée had taken to give birth, her blind gaze turned toward the once-miraculous Virgin whom she begged to put an end to her suffering.

Was it the odor of death that attracted all these females to her bedside? Arriving from a far-away village, distant relations, possible heirs, invaded her house and discussed her death while she was still alive. They gave orders, inquired about the smallest details of the funeral, indifferent to the fact that Aunt Rose could hear them. "Has someone thought about the shroud? And why are you waiting to order the coffin? Who will pay the priest? Has someone told him?" Her eyes bulging with fear, Aunt Rose did not recognize a single one of them. They were as foreign to her as the seagulls that had lined up on the rim of the pool and were filling the air with their moaning cries. For the first time, they had ventured far from the sea.

None of her tenants had come to her deathbed. Gathered in the courtyard, they were discussing whether they ought to offer a funeral wreath. My father, of course, would write the inscription for the ribbon. The estimated cost, divided by the number of households, seemed exorbitant. They took up the discussion on a new basis: a simple bouquet would replace the wreath.

The new result did not meet with unanimous approval. They separated without having reached a decision. Was it to lighten the so-heavy atmosphere of that day that Monsieur Alphonse made this suggestion:

—And why not the products of her own garden? I'm sure a bouquet of nettles would please her.

Death had struck twice in the same year: Renée and Rose. The letter R did not bring good luck to the inhabitants of the five houses crowded around the pool: you had been right to replace it with the letter L. Our two neighbors would perhaps be still alive if they had been called Lenée and Lose. Your mother announces the latter's death to you as soon as you arrive in the visiting room.

—The one who has the tango school? you ask in an unconcerned voice.

—Not at all, she says, annoyed. It's our landlady, who owns the house.

—The ownel of the tango school, you insist stubbornly. She's Blasilian.

—No! She's Cuban.

—It's the same thing, you reply dryly.

The two of you go around in circles; the air around you electrifies. Your mother notices and changes the subject. She tells you that Sea Eagle came in last, and with him the ruin of poor Rose. She died of it. You have no idea who or what Sea Eagle is: you don't see any connection between him and the life of our landlady, whom you continue to confuse with the Contessa.

Your mother tires you out. She only becomes tolerable when it's time for the gift parcels, which she produces one after another with the air of a magician:

—Guess what's inside!

You never guess.

—Doughnuts again! And I tell you time and time again that they make me puke!

—*But you liked them when you were little.*

—*I'm big now.*

To demonstrate to her, you climb up on a bench, and touch the ceiling with the palm of your hand.

She explains to you patiently that that's no reason not to like doughnuts. She has convinced you. There you are biting into the dough dripping syrup. You ask for more. She feeds you and makes conversation.

—*Everyone asks about you. It's really up to you to see them again. The doctor is willing to trust you to come home for a day or two.*

You reply that you wouldn't know what to say to all those people. It's so long since you left the neighborhood. And that's not mentioning the fact that now you have trouble putting on shoes. Your feet have swollen from always shuffling around in slippers.

You'd prefer not to leave.

—*I have my habits hele, my fliends.*

And your hand sweeps the space around you, up to the double security door and the main gate, after having scrupulously gone around the walls.

The calm of your conversation clashes with a sudden violence that makes you shiver. Your face becomes enflamed with a terrible rage. You advise your mother to shave her mustache and to dress in civilian clothing if she wants to see you again.

—*Soldiers are not much appleciated here. S.S. Nazis.*

You think you are speaking to your father: you realize this as you watch her pick up her things, then move away. You follow her, catch up with her before the door closes behind her. You dry her tears with the corner of your pajama jacket and cover her face with kisses. The countryside after rain, your mother's face. It only needs a ray of sun to light it up.

A glacial sun stood immobile above the five houses the day after Aunt Rose's funeral. A strange phenomenon, which my father attributed to opposing winds that tugged at it from either side, preventing it from advancing or retreating. It would have been impossible to contradict him. He would have become angry and refused to talk to us for a week. Winds, he went on, that come from the two opposite points of the planet, the first from the Sahara and the second from the west side of the Mediterranean, and that are called khamsin and mistral. The first strode across the desert, the second, across the sea, so that their gusts could cross above our roofs. Khamsin and mistral used our walls as an echo chamber to whistle in our ears and sweep away everything the local wind had piled up in corners. Two pots of basil placed at the lintels of the dead woman's door flew away in their turn toward an unknown destination.

The disappearance of the two plants moved the Contessa deeply, and she decreed three days of mourning. She owed at least that to the woman who had aided in the return of her dear Falstaff. Carlos Gardel was silenced for seventy-two hours, then replaced by the first movement of Beethoven's Fifth.

Subjected to a fate beyond their control, the students of the Universal Tango Institute had to measure their steps to the beat of destiny.

It was in this singular atmosphere that three armed individuals appeared in the neighborhood. Their kalashnikovs sowed panic and prevented Madame Latifa's hens from laying. Their camouflage uniforms, beards, and berets were not unknown to us. We had seen them in the newspapers.

—Che Guevara multiplied by three, said Mina.

They expressed themselves in a language not unlike that which emerged from the Contessa's gramophone. The one who seemed to be in charge took a key out of his pocket and fit it into Aunt Rose's lock. No one dared interfere. The dead woman's furniture departed through all the openings, and the holy picture, after a gliding flight, perched itself on the highest branch of the pomegranate tree.

My father tried to put a stop to the carnage, but had to retreat in his tracks when Aunt Rose's bed flew above his head. The furniture moving completed, the three fanatics flopped down not far from the pool, on what was left of a couch, and emptied bottles of beer, arak, and whiskey, which they proceeded to throw at our windows.

A delegation was formed. Followed by the four race-track brothers, preceded by the Contessa, pulled forcibly from her bed and obliged to serve as interpreter, my father demanded an explanation.

—You're crazy, howled the Contessa. You want an explanation from these bandits?

She became more explicit.

—Revolutionaries my ass, my mother's ass and my grandmother's and the asses of all the women of Cuba.

Inexhaustible Contessa. She, habitually so distinguished, was beside herself with rage. It was by revolutionaries of this sort that she had been despoiled of all her belongings, years earlier. They had occupied her hacienda, emptied the contents of her pantry and her wine cellar into their stomachs, smoked the acres of marijuana that her slaves had cultivated, hanged her husband, the brave Inocencio, and her lover, the dashing Augusto from the jacaranda tree; then they gave all her jewelry to their whores. There was nothing left for her to do but leave, go as far as possible from Cuba. Chance had brought her to our country. She had heard it spoken of by one of her tenant farmers. He had returned to Beirut with his savings, and had written her a long letter in which he informed her that he was going to marry a local beauty called Rose, and that he had built an "edificio" in the center of town. Finally, he asked her to look out for his son Candido, born of a liaison with a servant, whom he did not name, and with whom she did not concern herself.

Twenty years later, the Contessa had only to go to the return address on the letter when she arrived in Beirut.

The five dwellings built hastily around a putrid pool were of an extreme ugliness. As ugly as the aforementioned Rose, who was widowed in the meantime, and who never addressed a word to her. She held out to her, once a month, a hand into which the rent money dropped with a dry shuffling sound.

In fifteen years as neighbors, the Contessa had never found an occasion to say to Rose that she had known her late husband, and that she had not kept her promise concerning his illegitimate son.

Every evening, she would make up her mind to tell her everything the next day, but changed her mind when Rose's rooster woke her. When she saw Rose in her coffin, it was too late. Dead ears hear nothing. One might as well cry out in the desert.

Forty years later, I can still see the scene with extraordinary clarity. Five shivering men had taken shelter behind the back of a woman. Magnificently dignified in her nightdress, which swept the ground, the Contessa advanced, her head high despite her straggling chignon.

The procession gave rise to a thunderstorm of laughter. The three hoodlums were bent double. The five cowards and their Madonna demanded an explanation? Not a problem. They'd be served.

Of the sentences that flowed from the three mouths, the natives understood two words: *"Propriétario"* and *"Posesion."*

—*Posesion* of what, my father asked politely.

—Of all this, was the answer of the head of the band, indicating with a nonchalant wave of the hand the five houses and their inhabitants. He even had the impertinence to introduce himself.

—Candido, at your service.

We had all taken "Candido" to be an invention of Aunt Rose, a sort of scarecrow to back her up when she wanted to raise the rent! Candido, the illegitimate son of the long-defunct husband, this was he! He, the sole heir to the five miserable houses with their dovecotes and laundry rooms!

Was he planning to throw us all out into the street?

—He has the right, whispered the eldest of the racetrack brothers.

—We can discuss this, between people of the same world, suggested my father.

—*Mismo el mundo!* shouted Candido.

He, who had been joking, was transformed into a fury.

—*Un mundo de mierda!* he spat out. Candido pisses, shits, ejaculates on your houses, their tenants, your rents and their increases. He didn't leave Bolivia where he fought beside Guevara to collect the pennies of poor idiots who hide behind a woman's back. He is here for a noble cause: to destabilize the regime in power, a corrupt regime, and replace it with a revolutionary government, As for this shitty house, inherited from his shit of a father, it will serve as headquarters for the movement. I've said all there is to say!

They were about to leave when he let drop this sentence:

—Candido will blow everything up!

In the morning, we had made our decision. We would take refuge with Tantine in the mountains. We had all our lives to study. School could wait.

My father saw Beirut given over to the barbarians, thousands of dead. The newspapers that he pulled out from under his mattress showed Hiroshima.

—It's the same thing, more or less, he said, his finger moving across the photo from the mushroom cloud to the exploded houses and the bodies reduced to ash in the streets. He had succeeded in terrorizing us. The Vinikof children, who saw us with our suitcases at the bus stop, asked if we were leaving for the North Pole.

—We're going to Tantine's

—Does your Tantine live in Alaska? inquired the libidinous Youri at the sight of our sweaters, mufflers, and coats.

—What about school? asked Yara and Macha uneasily.

—We have all our lives to study.

When we went to Tantine's, we were used to a bi-colored village, brick red on top, green on the bottom. We had trouble even giving a name to the stretch of white that went from the mountain peak to the valley. Men, women, and children hid away in the burrows of their homes. The church bell and the town hall clock were muzzled by the frost. Living beings, nature, steel, all hibernated. The village seemed born out of some disquiet of the earth, of an illness that had struck its roads, its roofs, and even its cemetery, whose dead were now doubly buried under a thick layer of snow. It was by a series of slips and glides that we reached Tantine's house. The woman sitting motionless facing the fire that she kept feeding with sticks barely resembled the one we had left only three months earlier. Her staring at the flames had something distraught about it. Her life lost all its sense as soon as she stopped teaching. Teaching the alphabet to the peasant girl who kept house for her could not console her for the absence of her students, snowbound at home for three weeks now. Marie took the place of Tantine's inert limbs. She scoured the village to find food for her mistress. When it was necessary, she climbed the trees that the winter had spared to pluck from them things that were shaped like fruit, but lacked their flavor.

Tantine and Marie had heard nothing about Candido, and didn't want to think about the possibility of a civil war that would inflame the capital. They only knew that city-dwellers were unhappy in their heated houses, unhappy despite the running water, and the cars that took them from one place to another on roads that never were blocked by snow and ice.

Tireless Marie. Running nonstop between Tantine's house and the fields. She came back from shopping one morning in an excited state. Strangers come from no one knew where were pressing into service all the men of an age to bear arms. Trucks were there to transport them to the city, where there was fighting. What had been said to them to convince them to leave their families and their farms?

"Christians of the Orient!" one could read on a poster nailed to the church door. "You are menaced with extinction. You must fight for your survival and that of your children."

An identical poster, on the mosques of the capital, incited the Muslims to fight for their survival and that of their own children. Invisible hands were manipulating the simple and pushing them to kill each other. It was probably these same hands that had cleared the roads of snow overnight, had provided the weapons and opened hearts to hatred. A few hours later, the poet's tomb was burning like a torch. Their idol was being attacked. Those who had hesitated to go to the city joined the movement.

Marie's fiancé was one of these fighters. She was seen for the last time in the village square, next to the truck that was going to take him away. She disappeared. The whole village went in search of her. Hundreds of voices called out to her, all through the night, by the light of torches whose flashes streaked the mountain. Those who were scanning the valley thought they saw a red handkerchief near the riverbank. The men climbed back up with a jute sack stained with blood. A tibia pierced through one of its corners. No one dared open it: it was impossible to put that mass of flesh and bones in any order. Only the hand had stayed intact, a frozen pear held in its fingertips. One had only to look at the frozen tree that overhung the gully to know where it came from.

Death on the mountaintop; death on the coast. After Marie's burial, the village became unbearable to us. Tantine didn't try to hold us back; the disappearance of her guardian angel, as she called her, had paralyzed her. Our voyage back toward Beirut was interminable. We were stopped at one roadblock after another. Men in face masks, armed with kalashnikovs, searched the bus, our suitcases, our gazes, searching for the necessary sign that would class us with one camp or the other.

Our passage through the suburbs prepared us for the events that would bloody the country for fifteen years: men lined up against a wall, the rattle of gunfire, the bodies that slid down the buildings' façades to stop still in their own blood. Half the city had set itself up as judges, the other half as the accused. The country had come to a boiling point. Arafat, Carlos the terrorist, occupied the newspapers' front pages. Behind them, in profile, one could make out Candido, with his goatee and his beret on back to front.

Rose and Renée were forgotten. Our two neighbors had returned to the void, carried away by those invisible trains that slow down at the stations just long enough to choose their passengers. Renée and her eternal pile of ironing, Rose begging for her rent money. The only ones who died a natural death. As for the rest, a foot might have been found, a torso separated from its head, sometimes a finger circled by a wedding ring engraved with a date and two names. Impossible to identify the victims of explosions. The shreds of skin and clothing hanging from tree branches and the wrought iron of balconies could have belonged to anyone.

I have only to close my eyes to see them pass before me in line. The Contessa with her impeccable chignon, the veiled figure of Madame Latifa. Seven years ago, I ran into Roro Vinikof in the center of town. The siren that warned of a bombing prevented him from giving me news of his parents. I learned in half a sentence that his father had been killed by explosives he had been handling himself. After years of searching with shovels and pickaxes for the treasure the Armenian mage had told him of, he had graduated to dynamite, the only thing capable of overcoming the horde of devils that were driving him mad.

Perhaps you are one of those devils that kept mocking the engineer and his family, my brother. The Contessa, the Vinikofs, Aunt Rose, and all the others are absent from the pages you wrote. You never describe the neighborhood of your childhood in the small pile of papers shoved into a plastic bag that your mother faithfully keeps. A train already in motion, that's what you are. You traverse places and people without noticing them, without remembering them, without loving them.

Like a fist striking her chest, your portrait, that morning, on the cover of a magazine. Your mother recognized you despite the lack of resemblance between you and that sketch drawn on the corner of a table at La Palette by your friend Paul. A sketch ten years old, from the time when the English lady called you Rimbaud and passersby turned in their tracks to admire your beauty. How to explain the bandaged head, the hallucinated stare, that madman's stare, though you were no madman then? Had Paul seen into the future, seen the shriveled mouth through the voluptuous lips, the hollowed sockets through the dreamy gaze, and the black circles due to migraines after the electroshock treatments?

Contrary Mina might have disagreed, said the fellow on the cover wasn't her brother but Lazarus when he emerged from the tomb. But your three sisters have left the five houses around the stagnant pool. Everyone still in the neighborhood voices an opinion. The magazine passes from hand to hand. The portrait is commented on, not the article, laid out on a full page. The only one there who would have been capable of deciphering it abstains from doing so. Your father has deleted you from his thoughts. Madame Latifa, who does not understand the reason for so much hatred, beats her breast with her fists and mutters a prayer to Sitt Zeinab, the only saint capable of driving away the devil, the real creator of the drawing. The Vinikofs are perplexed. The devil, to them, is a treasure hunter, not an artist.

Your mother is convinced she can bring you back to

*your senses at the mere sight of these pages. Is it her fists
hammering the locked doors of the asylum or your name
cried out above the wall studded with fragments of broken
glass that open the gates to her? She knows that Wednesday
is the only visiting day, but what she has to do will broach
no delay. She is going to cure her boy. They bring you out in
pajamas before the gesticulating woman. You are asked to
listen to her. Your salvation will come from the two pages
that she is waving. Her hand extends the portrait to you,
trembling*

    —Do you recognize it? she asks you.

    You pout at her. Of course you recognize yourself.

    She asks you to read the article to her.

    —Slowly, so I don't miss anything.

    —I don't know how to lead now.

    *She throws in your face the ten years of school fees she
paid, then shows you her ruined hands. She could have
hired a maid.*

*In the pages that tell about you, spread out on her knees,
she deciphers a word here and a word there. She under-
stands them one by one, but loses her footing when it
comes to piecing together a whole sentence. She spells out
words and stumbles through the page. You pretend not to
hear. She knows she will have to manage on her own.*

    *"He comes toward me smiling, imperceptibly bent as
if his head were heavy to bear, always inclined toward
his shoulder. His oval face makes me think of Saint-
Exupéry . . ."*

    *She stops and stares at you as if she were seeing you
for the first time. She probably asks herself who is this
saint of whom she's never heard. Saint-Exupéry isn't an
Arab saint: she would have noticed his name on the calendar hanging behind the kitchen door.*

"A lunar face, eyes of still water whose lids never blink and a smooth forehead that holds strange secrets. The two hours that I just spent with V. S. were merely minutes slipping from one spurt of thought to another, from one place to another, although we had not budged from our seats. If a key exists to open V. S.'s soul, that key was lost in advance. Concrete references: he had been a journalist with Le Soir for two or three years when he was around twenty-one, discovered poetry at the age of fifteen. "Serious poems," he said, "because one's not yet mature." He advocates a return to the sources of poetry, that which needs neither inspiration nor ideas, which are merely mystification. V. S. moves among his paradoxes with ease, an ease at once fluid and obscure. But nothing is paradoxical for him, who wishes to join the great all and the great nothing. Who does he like to read? He admits to Rilke, after having juxtaposed the words orchard and asphalt, and books printed in Syrian and in Aramaic, because he does not know these two languages. He also loves trees. Not cedars, they are too old. He took a loathing to them after he learned that behind the hill of cedars that overhangs his mother's village there was another, even higher hill, and then a mountain, and more mountains behind that. Questioning him about his life in Paris where he spent a year will leave you frustrated. He says he found there only words and expressions emptied of their sense. The Europeans want to go everywhere, do everything. Sometimes I say to myself that they ought to come here to learn to do nothing."

Your mother gets up and brushes off her skirt. She can barely contain her anger. "Why did you lie to that woman? Since when do you read Syrian and Aramaic? And where did you meet her? Are you receiving guests now?"

The idea that the interview dates back several years

doesn't cross her mind. She demands an accounting from someone who has forgotten everything: the name of the journalist, the things he said to her, the place and the date of their meeting. His memory has kept only the hand of the painter sketching his portrait. He remembers with precision the color and the size of the pencil and how the lead broke each time he began to draw the head.

Then this sentence of Paul's, which is glued forever to the few memories that he retains: "Your brain, my young friend, gives off sparks."

April 1975. The civil war forced the asylum to free its patients. Their nurses and caretakers could no longer reach that suburb grown so lethal because of its geographical location between the coast and the mountains. The doors opened for the lunatics and amnesiacs who had forgotten even their given names, their family names, and the names of their natal villages. It was impossible to keep them. The shells being fired by Muslims and Christians, militias of the right and of the left, dedicated combatants and mercenaries, those shells killed at every blow.

A stony weight crushed the house at the announcement of your return. You were no longer part of the family. We were accustomed to knowing you were elsewhere, relieved that you seemed to be happy there. No object recalled your passage among us: your clothes, too large for you now, had been given to the poor; your books sold to the used bookshop on the corner; and your poems lost in that Paris which should have published them—and which had become your eldest sister's home.

Your mother, who comes through machine-gun fire to pick you up, covers half the distance by hitchhiking, half on foot. You wait for her without really waiting, crouched behind the giant gateway, in pajamas, ten years in the asylum has separated you from your clothing. You resist the hand that pulls you toward the exterior, you feel sheltered in this place, which has become familiar and homelike to you. For how long will the two of you try your forces against each other? Which of you will prevail? Her calls for help and your shrieks of terror are inaudible, the din coming from the sky drowns them out. She continues to call, no one hears her, the asylum's employees fled when the first bomb fell. Even the guard at the door has deserted his post.

You form a strange couple in the streets you pass through. The woman bent beneath the gesticulating man searches for a car, a truck, some vehicle that will relieve her of her burden. Militiamen in uniform point their kalashnikovs at the two figures who are moving toward the borderline between Muslim and Christian territories. You pass strange individuals: a paralytic in his wheelchair traveling swiftly, zigzagging to avoid partisans' bullets; farther on, a couple running toward the nearest cemetery. The little white coffin they carry on their heads contains their baby. The little body is tossed back and forth within it, with a sound like a rattle.

At home, you feel like a prisoner. Your father has removed the benevolent mask he wore for the last year; his face has taken on its old hostility. His step, in the living room where you've ended up, becomes deafening when he approaches you. You breathe better when he moves away. Your head pressed between your knees, you think you are invisible. In bed, where you spend your days and nights, you have a view of a spare of sky crisscrossed by rockets. Their impact on the façade of neighboring buildings makes you tremble while lighting up your face with a childish joy. For you, the war is a gigantic fireworks display.

You dream of the destruction of a world that betrayed you. Your pride comes back to you when news of massacres reaches your ears; it makes no difference in which sector, you belong to no community, no movement.

You choose the most violent bombings as the time to take a walk. The tall fellow who paces swiftly up and down the streets becomes a target for the partisans. Hit twice in the legs, never in the head, you go your way, jumping in your plaster cast, alone with your shadow that precedes you in the morning, follows you in the afternoon, shrinks into a dark stain beneath your soles when noon nails itself to your half-bald skull. You have forbidden your mother to follow you or to call out your name from the window. You come back when you are good and ready, when your nostrils have breathed in the odor of gunpowder till you are drunk with it, and when the din of war has replaced that of the machines that crashed into your head.

Ten years in the asylum. After the tenth, you stopped counting. You come back to a neighborhood in ruins. By what miracle is the house of your suffering still standing? It scorns you and prevents the forgetfulness necessary for you to be at peace. The cracked walls hold themselves back from falling. The same cracks in the mirror above the washbasin. Your face divided in two, like your spirit. You transmit your unease with life to everything you touch. The faucet spits water violently into your face, and the lamp blinks, ready to give up the ghost. Wrapped up to the neck in a moth-eaten blanket that protects you, you say, from malevolent waves, you watch your childhood and then your adolescence pass by against a background of rubble and nettles. A dog barking far away, wheels that bite into the asphalt, drill into your brain where four winters follow one after the other, with their storms, their torrential rains, then those inexplicable silences that have the whiteness of cemeteries.

You were convinced, when your mother made you get down from her back, that she had stopped in front of the wrong house, while the change came from what surrounded it: the empty space reflected on the walls gave the impression that it had turned around on its foundation. You are so impoverished in memories and landmarks. Don't even try to compare. However, you know quite a few things: among others, that the neighborhood is located at the highest point of the city, that its streets descend toward the sea. But it sometimes happens that you reverse people and events. Mademoiselle Renée died of a brain tumor, old Aunt Rose in childbirth, the four racetrack brothers had left for Bolivia. They were battling beside Che Guevara for reasons that seemed obscure to you. How could your head retrieve its images? Would you have to make time run backwards?

You are fifteen again. You write poems that make your sister melt with emotion but displease your father. To emerge unscathed from this story, to escape the asylum, the electroshock treatments, the barefoot flights into the night, the humiliating homecomings when no one was waiting for you, standing in the doorway, you have only one solution. You must submit your poems to your father, ask his advice, involve that policeman, enemy of the imagination, in the process, make him think that poetry would benefit from his imprimatur.

What lassitude on your features! Pulling the past by its hair to drag it backwards with its horde of the living and the dead is useless. Time does not turn inside out like a glove, and human beings cannot be thrown again and again like dice. And furthermore, they have all disappeared from your life. No one calls you, no one asks for news of you, and those who pass you in the street don't recognize you. You have changed. Your once-sensual mouth is reduced to a slit, and the two burning coals of your gaze are extinguished, replaced by two marbles that turn in their sockets. Your only friend: the evening. It brings a great peace to your face. You revel in the semi-darkness, the sleep of the walls, trees, and mirrors. An old man of thirty.

You are defeated. Here you are exhausted, emptied of any love, any hatred, any desire, any rancor. Your body is like an empty violin case. Through it, one can hear the wind. The curse of the monastery that your mother told of again and again extends as far as La Palette. A spark lights up in your eyes at the mention of that name. Do you know that that mythical spot was razed by bullets and shrapnel, and that many of the poets and painters who frequented it now inhabit cemeteries?

The poet Antoine Mechahwar hanged himself in his attic.

The poet Fouad Gabriel Naffah: dead of poverty and hunger. His body was found, decomposed, fifteen days later.

Your friend Paul Guiragossian, also dead after an elevator crushed his leg.

You are the only survivor.

AFTERWORD

Fifty years later, I can still hear the screaming of my poet brother, as he was dragged toward the ambulance by two orderlies from the asylum. Fifty years later, in all my nightmares, I see the nettles that surrounded the house of my childhood thrust up from the parquet and invade my apartment in Paris, wind themselves around the furniture, around my feet.

How can one cure the obsessions born of a childhood crushed by a tyrannical father who proclaimed night after night that his son should be buried alive because he wrote poems; by a silenced mother who could not save her son and seemed not to notice her daughters' distress?

And what became of my childhood neighborhood? For years, I asked myself that nightly, in front of the television that broadcast images of the war ravaging my country. Was the house among the nettles still standing? I learned, reading the newspaper, that the more prosperous building adjacent to ours, which had been commandeered as the headquarters of the Phalangist party, was blown up by an enemy militia. Four stories toppled like a pack of cards: one hundred militiamen of the Phalange dead, along with their chief, Bechir Gemayel, who had just been elected president of the country—and, killed as well, a distant cousin and her young son, simply tenants of an apartment on the top floor.

A neighborhood drenched in blood. Had the pomegranate tree that dripped its red juice on our doorstep presaged all this violence? More courageous than I was, my two sisters went back to the neighborhood once the war was over. I couldn't do it. Each time I returned to Beirut, I would begin to walk toward what had been our home, curious to know if its walls had survived the war's violence, and then find myself turning, going back the way I came.

What became of our neighbors? Were they all killed in the war? I've never seen one of them at the talks and readings I give when I've been invited back to Lebanon. Are they dead, or simply not interested? To see me again would bring back to them our nocturnal cries, the catastrophic midnight awakenings when they would arrive with buckets of water to extinguish the fire from the oil lamp that a furious gesture of my father's had broken. That accursed lamp, it does me no good to detest it, it reappears in my poems as if to remind me that the past can't be wiped away with a rag.

Still, a kind of cure has come to me through writing. I took over from my brother, condemned to thirty years' imprisonment in an asylum, his memory erased by electroshock treatments. I wrote the poems he could no longer write, at first with his pen in his notebook, before telling the story of his ordeal in this book.

A House at the Edge of Tears, written after the death of both my father and mother, has a double, a novel written in Arabic by my sister. Now a well-known journalist and novelist in Lebanon, May Menassa, the most silenced of the three of us, described, in her book, the same scenes of violence, the same descent into madness. Was it our brother who opened the road of writing to us? Three girls and a boy lived in a house surrounded by nettles. Locked up unjustly by his father, when he was not mad, but depressed, and later addicted, the boy had all his links with writing cut. The three girls took his place. I write in French; May writes in Arabic; our youngest sister Layla—Mina in this story—translates from French to Arabic. We hope the dead poet (he died five years ago) applauds us from his grave.

Vénus Khoury-Ghata
Paris, 2004

VÉNUS KHOURY-GHATA is a Lebanese poet and novelist, resident in France since 1973, author of many collections of poems and novels. She received the Prix Mallarmé in 1987 for *Monologue du mort,* the Prix Apollinaire in 1980 for *Les Ombres et leurs cris,* and the Grand Prix de la Société des gens de lettres for *Fables pour un people d'argile* in 1992. Her *Anthologie personnelle,* a selection of her previously published and new poems, was published in Paris by Actes Sud in 1997. Her most recent collection, *Quelle est la nuit parmi les nuits,* was published by Mercure de France in 2004. Her work has been translated into Arabic, Dutch, German, Italian, and Russian, and she was named a Chevalier de la Légion d'Honneur in 2000.

MARILYN HACKER is a winner of a National Book Award in Poetry and the author of eleven books, including *Winter Numbers,* which received a Lambda Literary Award and the Lenore Marshall Award in 1995; *Selected Poems,* which was awarded the Poets' Prize in 1996; and the verse novel, *Love, Death, and the Changing of the Seasons.* Her latest collections are *Desesperanto* and *First Cities: Collected Early Poems.* She is a noted translator, most recently of *Birds and Bison* by Claire Malroux and *She Says* by Vénus Khoury-Ghata. Marilyn lives in New York and Paris and is currently Professor of English at City College.

A House at the Edge of Tears has been set in Apollo, a typeface designed by Adrian Frutiger in 1962. Book design by Wendy Holdman. Composition at Stanton Publication Services, Inc. Manufactured by Friesens on acid-free paper.